19

D1320927

Iron Eyes the Spectre

Having delivered the body of wanted outlaw Mason Holt to the sheriff at Diablo Creek, infamous bounty hunter Iron Eyes collapses, badly wounded, and his would-be sweetheart Squirrel Sally desperately tries to find a doctor to help him.

However, unknown to Sally, she is heading into a dangerous and uncharted desert where a mysterious tribe of Indians live. Then when Holt's older brothers discover their sibling is dead, they vow revenge and set out after the man who killed him. Soon both outlaws and Indians alike realize how dangerous Iron Eyes is.

Iron Eyes the Spectre

Rory Black

A Black Horse Western

ROBERT HALE

© Rory Black 2017
First published in Great Britain 2017

ISBN 978-0-7198-2565-1

The Crowood Press
The Stable Block
Crowood Lane
Ramsbury
Marlborough
Wiltshire SN8 2HR

www.bhwesterns.com

Robert Hale is an imprint
of The Crowood Press

Typeset by
Derek Doyle & Associates, Shaw Heath
Printed and bound in Great Britain by
CPI Group (UK) Ltd, Croydon, CR0 4YY

Dedicated to my dear friend Maxine Hansen

PROLOGUE

This was a silent place. A place where the prairie filled the ancient canyons between rises of mountainous peaks. Jagged spires of crimson rocks defied the elements and gravity and pointed to the equally quiet heavens. Monstrous mesas rose up into the air like scarlet giants and loomed over everything below their unequalled heights.

Few, if anyone, apart from the various tribes of nomadic Indians, who still controlled the majority of this territory, had ever ventured into this devilish land. Even fewer had survived to tell the tale.

From their perilous perches above the parched canyon a hundred eyes watched the progress of the uninvited intruder as it forged a path between Joshua trees and sagebrush, oblivious to the wrath and danger it was incurring.

The weathered stagecoach was not on any sched-
uled route for this was a place that only led to Hell.
Its driver did not work for any of the various trans-
port companies who plied their trade through the
vast regions known as the West. Dust rose up from
the hoofs of its team into the dry haze and drifted
toward the blue cloudless sky as the young woman
frantically whipped the sturdy team of six black
horses.

With gritted teeth and determined eyes, Sally
Cooke drove her team of valiant horses through the
canyon and out toward the lifeless desert.

As the intrepid female urged the horses on, she
was totally unaware of the numerous braves who
watched from the hidden shadows of the high rocks.

The only thought in the mind of young Sally was
to find help. Help for her unconscious cargo. For
inside the belly of the stagecoach lay the infamous
bounty hunter known throughout the vast heartland
of the West as Iron Eyes – the hideously scarred man
she loved even though her feelings were unrequited.

Totally lost, the golden-haired Sally had no idea of
where she was heading or the deadly interest of her
unseen onlookers as they noted the progress of the
stagecoach.

The noonday sun filled the canyon with its blistering heat as the six-horse team continued to obey the

commands of their tiny mistress and ploughed on.

If Sally had spared the time to look over her shoulder at the high mesas, she would have seen the white plumes of smoke rising from the scarlet peaks. Long before the invention of the telegraph, the plains Indians had sent messages across vast distances to instantly communicate with one another.

Sally did not know it, but her naïve intrusion into the land of blood-coloured rocks had already been noted. Every single warrior within the uncharted territory already knew of the stagecoach and its driver with the golden mane.

Every fibre in her petite form told her that she had to keep going if she were going to find help for her beloved Iron Eyes. Then Sally noticed something far out in the distance ahead of her horses.

A dazzling series of lights from beyond the sickening heat haze caught her attention and suddenly seemed to justify her actions to keep going and not turn back.

'A town,' Sally reasoned. 'I was right. I knew there had to a town out here someplace.'

She cracked her bullwhip over the heads of her team.

The stagecoach forged on into the jaws of Hell.

ONE

The mysterious bounty hunter known throughout the west as Iron Eyes had slept for more than a day inside the body of the stagecoach as it journeyed toward the distant lights of the unknown settlement ahead. The gaunt, emaciated figure was suffering from total exhaustion and blood loss. After locating a town and collecting the reward money for his latest prize, both Iron Eyes and his companion Squirrel Sally had set out on the trail back to Texas. She drove her battle-scarred stagecoach as he had ridden his high-shouldered mount beside the lead horse of her team.

Yet after less than twenty-four hours of heading into an uncharted prairie, Iron Eyes had suddenly buckled and fallen from his magnificent palomino stallion.

Squirrel Sally had grown used to her 'betrothed' looking more dead than alive and had not given his gaunt appearance a second thought until he had silently slid from his saddle and crashed into the unforgiving sand.

For what had seemed like an eternity, Sally had thought that the man she was besotted with was dead. His long black mane of hair was spread out from his tortured features. No corpse had ever looked as bad as the bounty hunter did to the alarmed female.

The only sign that Iron Eyes still lived was a vein in his temple that visibly throbbed with every beat of his black heart.

Only after Sally had somehow found the strength to drag him into her stagecoach, and plied him with enough whiskey for his eyes to open again, had she noticed the savage wound hidden beneath his long trail coat. The brutal wound had still been pumping blood when the determined female had cleaned and sewn his flesh back together.

A bullet had hit him, carved a trail through his pitifully lean body and then exited out of his back. His dark red shirt and blood-stained trail coat had concealed his injuries from Sally's prying eyes.

'You dumb ass,' Sally scolded.

Iron Eyes silently winked and then gave a sigh.

11

Only then had the man known to his enemies as the living ghost fallen into the deep sleep his body craved. His long skeletal body was propped between the sacks of horse feed and a ten-gallon barrel of water in the interior of the stagecoach.

His scarred head rocked back and forth as Sally steered her team of six large black horses. Iron Eyes was oblivious to everything as his body fought against his savage injuries. Injuries that would have killed most men.

For the first time since she had first encountered the infamous bounty hunter, Sally was fearful that Iron Eyes might be losing his long battle with the Grim Reaper.

She had never seen him look so helpless before and it frightened the normally feisty Sally. She whipped the long leathers across the backs of her team and encouraged them on toward the distant lights.

There was urgency in her wrists.

She had to get her beloved 'man' to a doctor as fast as she could. The team of six powerful horses responded to their mistress and moved swiftly across the sand to where Sally was convinced she could see lantern light.

Yet no matter how hard she whipped her team of charging horses, the lights did not appear to get any closer. After more than an hour of racing across the vast desert, the disheartened female eased back on her long reins and pushed her bare right foot against the brake pole.

A cloud of dust rose up into the air as the six lathered-up horses came to an abrupt halt. As the dust settled, Sally picked up her primed corncob pipe and chewed on its stem thoughtfully. Her tiny hands wrapped the long leathers around the pole and then she scratched a match against her thigh. A flame erupted and she sucked it into the tobacco filled bowl.

As smoke billowed from her handsome face, Sally pondered her situation. This was totally different to the way things usually went, she thought. She lifted her Winchester and pushed down on its hand guard before looking into its magazine.

Her trusty rifle was fully loaded and ready should she need it. Her handsome eyes looked around the desolation of her surroundings from her high perch atop the driver's seat. The sun was low in the sky and the shadows grew longer with every beat of her throbbing heart.

Normally she would be chasing Iron Eyes, trying to catch up with him. Sally was used to that and had never given a second thought as to why the fearless bounty hunter was so intent on trying to shake her

13

off his trail, but this was totally different.

Smoke drifted from her lips. For all she knew, Iron Eyes was lying dead inside the belly of the coach. A cold shiver traced her spine as she held on to the brake pole and started down toward the ground.

'You better not be dead,' Sally nervously said as her hand reached up and twisted the door handle. 'I ain't busting my back burying you.'

Reluctantly she pulled the door open and climbed up into the interior of the stagecoach. It was stifling inside the confines of the coach as Sally moved closer to the motionless bounty hunter.

Her keen eyes studied him and only when she placed a hand on his chest could she feel his heart still beating. Sally chewed on the stem of her pipe and shook her head. The normally intrepid Iron Eyes looked worse than she had ever seen him and utterly helpless.

Sally wondered what she should do.

She swung around on her threadbare pants and dropped her legs back out of the coach door. Her mind raced in search of answers. Normally she just chased the bounty hunter as he fled her unwanted advances, but now it was she who had to make the decision of what their next move ought to be.

She sucked the last dregs of smoke from her pipe and then tapped its bowl against the body of the stagecoach and watched as the smouldering ash fell over her dangling feet.

'Think, Sally gal,' she muttered to herself as she glanced over her shoulder at the unconscious Iron Eyes. 'What should I do? It's hard to tell how damn sick that skinny galoot is. He always looks like that.'

She considered her options.

There seemed to be no right answer. She glanced at the darkening sky and then squinted straight at the setting sun. It was clear by her reading of the elements that there was merely an hour of daylight remaining. Sally looked straight ahead to where she could have sworn she had seen the lights of a town.

She straightened up to her full five feet and shook her head. Her golden locks caught the rays of the setting sun as her sharp mind considered the dilemma. The lights were no longer visible.

'Where the hell have they gone?' she spat before hauling the sack of grain from inside the coach and carrying it to the horses. After spreading the team's rations on the ground she walked back and then emptied what was left before the tall palomino tethered to the tailgate. As she went to fill a bucket with water from the barrel inside the coach, she paused again and stared to where she was convinced the lights had been. They were still gone. 'Now that's weird. Damn weird.'

Sally finished watering the horses and then checked Iron Eyes for the umpteenth time. The long-legged bounty hunter was still in a deep sleep. She slammed the door and then clambered up the side of the stagecoach with the agility of someone who still had the benefit of youth on her side. Sally threw her leg on to the roof and scrambled up after it. She then straightened up. The surface of the wooden roof was hot under her bare feet as she walked to the driver's seat and stepped down on to it.

The perplexed female rubbed her eyes and uncoiled the reins from around the brake pole. She released the pole and then slapped the long leathers.

'Get moving,' Sally shouted. 'There's a town out there and I intend finding it.'

The powerful horses sprang into action and took the strain of the hefty vehicle. The stagecoach began to move again through the expanse of sand. Chains rattled as the six black horses gathered pace and responded to the urging of the feisty female on the driver's seat.

The sound of the bullwhip cracking in the air was like rapid gunfire. The muscular team were soon up to speed as Sally guided them straight ahead.

She knew where she had last noticed the alluring lights and doggedly kept her horses heading in that direction. Her weary mind could not understand

16

what was happening and wished that she could ask Iron Eyes to give her some much-needed advice.

Yet he was still totally unconscious.

Then as the shadows lengthened her keen eyesight once again spotted the flickering lights in the distance. The thoughtful female bit her lower lip and frowned.

'What the hell's going on here?' she wondered.

She gripped her long leathers in one hand and then rested her trusty rifle on her lap. As the horses continued moving deeper into the unknown, Sally's index finger stroked the Winchester's trigger.

'If some galoot is messing with me,' she silently warned. 'They'd best be ready to die. I ain't in the mood to take prisoners.'

TWO

The rattling stagecoach had travelled another five miles through the arid terrain as the merciless sun slowly began to set. The fearless female had noticed that the high spires of jagged rock had spread out as the prairie gave way to the smooth expanse of sand. The canyon was now nothing but sand dunes. The desert grew darker as Sally cracked her bullwhip above her head and urged the exhausted team on to where she could still see the strange elusive lights sparkling like diamonds in the distant shadows.

Whatever it was out there, it was luring her like a moth to a naked flame and she knew it. Sally was helpless to resist the draw of the hypnotic lights and unable to fathom what they were exactly. All she could tell for certain was that they were not natural.

They had to be lights, she told herself. Either

street or house lights. Yet the further she travelled toward them, the more she began to doubt her own sanity.

There was definitely something out there flashing or dazzling at her like a beacon. Sally shook her head and rubbed the sand from her face.

She curled her toes against the rim of the driver's box, leaned forward and screamed at the black horses below her. The desert was getting colder as the heat from the sun slowly faded and the shadows melted into the dunes.

A chill in the air seemed to drill right through her flesh and burrow into her bones. But she felt that there was no time to stop and drag out the undertaker's frock coat that Iron Eyes had given her from the canvas-covered boot.

Somewhere deep inside her head a haunting voice kept telling her to keep going and find someone who could help her companion.

In search for inspiration, Sally glanced heavenward for a brief moment. Night had arrived far faster than she had anticipated.

There was no moon. Just a million stars set against the blackest of skies like precious jewels adorning a black velvet drape. The words of advice that Iron Eyes had once bestowed upon her and repeated for the previous twelve months kept filling her mind as she encouraged the team on toward the mysterious illumination.

A moonless sky was good for the hunted but bad for the hunter. Until this very moment, Sally had not even known what that meant.

Now she knew.

If there was anyone out there ready and willing to try and assassinate her, Sally knew that she would not be an easy target.

The moonless sky would protect her for a while.

Sally shivered again and plucked a half bottle of whiskey from the box at her feet. She pulled its cork with her teeth, spat and then lifted the bottle to her lips. The hard liquor burned its way down into her innards as she whipped her team with her left hand.

The remaining content was devoured in three long gulps and fumes filled her head, but it did not drive the cold from her bones.

Sally threw the empty bottle into the darkness as the stagecoach ploughed on toward the lights which still seemed to get no closer.

Although she was unafraid, Sally was cautious. Iron Eyes had taught her that it always paid to be cautious. He never feared anything, not even death itself, but he was always wary of things he could not see.

With the skill of an acrobat, Sally patted the inside

of the deep box until her bare foot located her tobacco pouch. She lifted it and then grabbed it with her fingers. Without taking her eyes off the distant lights, Sally managed to pull the drawstring and pull out a small thin cigar and a match.

As the stagecoach jolted up and down and swayed like a drunken dog, the tiny female suddenly became aware that she was vulnerable sitting so high off the ground.

Her beautiful eyes darted around the desert in search for the danger she felt was close. Then she struck the match with her thumbnail and just managed to light the cigar before the breeze extinguished the flickering flame.

Sally sucked frantically until she managed to fill her lungs with smoke. She closed her eyes for a brief moment to savour the satisfied feeling that engulfed her.

Her pleasure was short-lived. It lasted only until she opened her eyes again.

The sight that greeted her caused her to press her foot hard against the brake-pole. She sound of the stagecoach brakes screaming echoed through the darkness. As the vehicle beneath her rocked on its springs, Sally stared in disbelief to where the lights had been.

Yet again, they were gone.

Sally looped the long leathers around the pole and then rested her knuckles on her shapely hips. She shook her head and then scratched her wavy mane.

'Now that just ain't possible,' she shouted angrily. 'One minute there's a town out yonder and then there ain't and then there is and then. . . .'

Angrily she spat the cigar at the sand and then leapt from the high driver's board. The sand was still soft but no longer hot. She moved to the coach and dragged its door open again. The floor of the stage-coach was wet where water had splashed during the hectic ride, but it was not the water that she was looking at.

It was her beloved man.

Sally clambered up into the coach and entered. She placed her hand on his temple. He was hot. Too hot.

'That don't feel right,' Sally reasoned. 'Iron Eyes has got a fever brewing. He's burning up.'

She sat on the wet floor beside the motionless bounty hunter and wondered what she ought to do for the best. The trouble was that Sally had never been faced with a problem like this before.

As she pondered whether she should try and cool him down or maybe light a campfire to warm him up, she heard something out in the vast ocean of sand.

It was a noise that sounded like a coyote, but Sally had never heard of any coyotes hunting in the middle of arid deserts. Her eyes tightened in her head as she stared out into the starlit dunes.

Another more troubling notion came to her.

What if it were someone trying to sound like a coyote?

She gulped as a sudden realization gripped her. Indians were said to call out to one another using sounds that imitated various animals or birds.

Sally moved away from her unconscious Iron Eyes and edged closer to the open door of the coach. She rolled over on to her knees and knelt staring out into the eerie starlight.

'Whatever that is, I sure hope it ain't Injuns,' she muttered to herself before reaching to Iron Eyes' blood-stained trail coat and fishing one of his Navy Colts from its deep pockets.

The six-shooter was far heavier than she had imagined it and far more awkward to handle than her trusty rifle. Sally placed both thumbs on its hammer and vainly tried to pull it back into a cocked position. It was useless, she fumed angrily, and returned the hefty weapon to his pocket. Sally needed her trusty rifle, she thought. She was a crack-shot with any type of rifle, but virtually pitiful with most handguns.

Faster than spit, Sally swung out of the interior of

the stagecoach and climbed up its side. Her small hand grabbed the luggage railing and hauled herself upward. She clambered on to the roof's flat surface and crawled toward the front of the vehicle.

She reached down and plucked her Winchester off the driver's seat and then swung around with the deadly repeating rifle in her hands.

Suddenly another chilling animal call echoed from out in the dunes. Sally had only just turned to where the strange sound had emanated when its howling was answered from behind her back. She rolled over and over across the roof until she was looking through the railing at the rear of the coach.

Sally rested on her belly. Her well-formed bosom prevented her from getting as flat as she would have liked.

'Damn these chests,' she complained. 'It's like trying to hunker down on two damn puppies.'

She squinted hard at the starlit dunes. Her eyes darted around the dimly lit ocean of rolling sand but she could not see anyone. A bead of sweat rolled from her golden waves and dripped on to the cocked and readied rifle.

More unnerving howls echoed around the stationary stage as Sally rubbed her nervous brow with her naked arm. She swallowed hard and began to accept the fact that it had to be Indians.

24

'They're getting closer by the sound of it,' she hissed under her breath. 'Whoever them critters are, they're heading this way.'

She shook her mane of wild hair.

'Damn that selfish Iron Eyes,' she cursed. 'That skinny bastard sure could be useful around now. He wouldn't have to do no shooting, all he'd have to do is let them varmints see him. His ugly features would give them the willies.'

Sally leaned over the railings and shouted into the stagecoach. 'Wake up, you ornery bonehead. Your betrothed could sure use some help about now, darling.'

There was no response. The bounty hunter was still sleeping like a baby and totally unaware of the potential danger that was getting alarmingly close to the long stationary vehicle.

It was becoming clear to the fiery female that if Iron Eyes did not awaken from his delirium soon, he might never be able to do so. Sally had always relied upon her beloved Iron Eyes when it came to the various tribes they had encountered since she had first started travelling with him.

Most tribes were usually hostile to the strange bounty hunter, yet not all of them. Sally wished that she was more knowledgeable about them.

She sniffed the air in a desperate attempt to locate

the men that she knew were moving closer yet she was still unable to spot with her keen eyesight.

'Them critters must be downwind,' she frowned.

The words had barely left her lips when another sound filled the arid terrain. The high-pitched noise grew louder until an arrow embedded itself into the wooden edge of the stagecoach roof a mere inch below the metal luggage railing.

Sally's eyes widened. The pulsating arrow had only just narrowly missed its target and she knew it.

'That was too close,' she raged before leaping to her feet and racing back to the driver's seat. Without missing a step she crossed the lengthy stagecoach roof and jumped down into the box.

A flurry of arrows came hurtling from out of the darkness and passed over the box as she ducked down. It was clear that she was the target and that did not sit well with her. She poked the long rifle barrel over the edge of the box and squeezed its trigger. A deafening blast sent a flame out into the darkness.

'Eat my lead, you sand-sucking varmints,' Sally growled before staggering to the opposite side of the stage and firing her rifle again. 'You can't scare me with your damn toothpicks. I'm an ornery critter and I don't die easy.'

Another volley of arrows suddenly flew through the air like a flurry of crazed hornets. They peppered the

26

side of the stagecoach with such force, the vehicle rocked under the impact. Knowing that the next barrage of lethal missiles might land amid her precious horses and cause carnage, she decided to act.

Sally freed the reins, released the brake pole and whipped the team. She frantically screamed at the horses and then ducked down into the box as the stagecoach began to move.

The team bounded forward and within seconds were thundering through the dunes at breakneck speed. As the black horses thundered into the darkness amid another torrent of arrows, Sally crouched in the driver's box and began blasting her rifle at the still unseen archers.

With the stagecoach hurtling even deeper into the unknown terrain, Sally could hear countless arrows striking the woodwork of her battle-bruised vehicle. She realized that she had to get the team moving faster if she were to escape the deadly attack. She dropped her smoking Winchester, swung around and then collected the loose reins in her hands.

She lashed the backs of her racing team again and kept the powerful animals ploughing forward. Then something caught her attention. Sally looked to the distant lights. Her hands gripped the edge of the driver's box as she stared through the starlit sand dunes.

Whatever they were, she thought, they were getting brighter and a lot bigger. A cold shiver traced down her spine. It had nothing to do with the falling temperature.

Sally was scared.

THREE

Diablo Crest had been constructed on the very edge of the land it had been named after. The two dozen red brick and wooden buildings had been sapped of every drop of moisture in the decades since they had been first built. The monstrous mesas loomed over the desolate and remote settlement, defying anyone to venture into the desert canyons that separated them.

None of the townspeople of Diablo Crest ever dared enter the mysterious land for it was said that the Devil himself dwelled there amid his blood-coloured towering spires. Some of the more imaginative citizens even thought that the desert was the gateway to Hell.

Only strangers unfamiliar to its infamous reputation ever made the mistake of travelling south into

29

the arid and uncharted terrain. For, as everyone in Diablo Creek knew only too well, those that went in, never came back out.

The scarlet spires of jagged rock pointed up into the cloudless heavens like accusing fingers. After Iron Eyes had claimed the two thousand dollar bounty on outlaw Mason Holt's lifeless body, he had quickly left the area alongside Squirrel Sally's stage-coach.

Yet unknown to his feisty female companion, Iron Eyes had been severely wounded before his deadly accuracy had brought Mason Holt down.

Sally had guided her stagecoach beside the man she was besotted with and not realized until it was too late that the infamous bounty hunter was badly wounded. Iron Eyes had automatically mounted his majestic palomino stallion in Diablo Creek and started riding as his pitifully lean frame bled and bled.

Mile after mile, Iron Eyes had battled with his own delirium and was totally unaware that he was leading the trusting Sally into a place where even he would never willingly venture.

That had been two days before the three riders slowly approached the sun-baked Diablo Creek in search of their fellow outlaw and sibling.

Sunlight raced across the dusty town as dawn

abruptly arrived. Its inhabitants stopped going about their daily rituals and looked out toward the trio of horsemen as they approached through the morning mist.

The dust-caked riders looked like ghosts as the shimmering dew was sucked from the ground and swirled around the lathered up horses beneath them.

Mason Holt's three brothers had arranged a month before to meet him in the remote settlement. As they approached, they recognized his horse standing outside the small sheriff's office. It belonged to the youngest of the Holt brothers.

Delmer Holt was the oldest of the outlaw's siblings and had been rustling steers throughout Texas and its adjoining territories for more than a decade. His brothers Caleb and Spike were a handful of years younger and had joined Delmer after a few failed attempts on their own. Delmer had proven a skilful rustler and commanded top prices for the cattle he drove south of the border. The trio of outlaws had become wanted less than a year after they had joined forces and had sizable bounties on their heads. They had only allowed their baby brother Mason to join their well-oiled outfit a matter of ten months earlier. They knew the youngster was more of a liability than an asset but he was kin and Delmer tolerated the far younger Holt sibling against his better judgement.

The sound of their jangling spurs alerted the inhabitants of Diablo Creek to their arrival long before the morning mist cleared. Delmer was used to the curious eyes that always greeted them when they entered a new town and paid little notice to it. He only watched out for star-packing lawmen with itchy trigger fingers.

As the Holt brothers entered the outskirts of the bleached settlement, they were quick to spot their brother's tethered horse. The disconcerting fact that the horse had obviously spent the night tied to the hitching pole outside the sheriff's office did not sit well in Delmer's always alert mind. He had taught his far younger sibling that it did not pay to draw the attention of men with tin stars pinned to their shirts. As usual, Mason seemed to have ignored the advice.

'Look,' Delmer pointed a finger as his mount led Caleb and Spike down the middle of the main street. 'There's his buckskin.'

Both Spike and Caleb shook their heads at the sight.

'That young fool has tied his horse up outside the sheriff's office, boys,' Caleb sighed heavily. 'That kid never realizes you just can't do that when you got bounty on your damn head.'

'That boy sure is spunky,' Spike chuckled as he trailed his brothers toward the mount. 'Only Mason

32

would have the guts to do that.'

'That ain't guts, Spike,' Delmer argued as he teased his reins. 'That's stupidity. A halfwit would know better. Mason's gonna get us killed one of these damn days.'

Caleb nodded agreement as Spike shrugged.

Delmer Holt rubbed the trail grime from his unshaven features and then spat at the ground as his eyes darted at the faces that observed their every move. As he focused on the gathering crowd to either side of the street, he observed that none of them were armed. A wry smile crept across his unshaven features.

'Keep your eyes peeled for the sheriff, boys,' he said in a breathless tone. 'The last thing we want is to run into an ambitious lawman.'

Spike pulled one of his six-shooters from its holster and rested it on his saddle horn in readiness. 'If I see a sheriff packing a scattergun, I'll send him into early retirement, Delmer.'

Their three mounts were turned toward the small sheriff's office and the horse they knew belonged to their younger brother. Delmer straightened up on his saddle as his eyes studied the buckskin gelding and the situation they were facing.

'I don't like this,' Delmer admitted to the surprise of his younger siblings. 'Something's wrong here.'

Caleb looked nervously at Delmer.

'What you mean?' he asked as he stared at his grim-faced elder. 'What could be wrong?'

Delmer gave a tilted nod at Mason's horse.

'The kid's green but even Mason wouldn't leave his nag saddled up all night outside a lawman's office,' he observed. 'I taught him better than that.'

All three horsemen eased back on their reins and stopped their mounts at the hitching pole next to their brother's beleaguered buckskin gelding.

Delmer threw his long left leg over his saddle cantle and then lowered his long frame to the parched sand. He gathered up his reins and then secured them to the pole.

'I've got a gut feeling about this,' Delmer said as he patted the neck of his trail-weary mount. 'And it don't feel good.'

Caleb looked at the townsfolk who were watching their every action. 'We're sure drawing a crowd, Delmer. I don't like this one bit. We should ride out of here while we still can.'

Delmer shook his head. 'We agreed to meet Mason here. We can't go until we've found his sorrowful hide.'

Never one to argue with his older brother, Caleb just chewed on the tails of his bandanna and watched the watchers.

Spike hastily dismounted and looped his long leathers around the twisted hitching pole. He removed his hat and then wiped his forehead with his grubby jacket sleeve.

'Mason's just a kid, Delmer,' he said as he ducked under the pole and stepped up on to the boardwalk where Delmer was standing like a statue. 'He probably found himself a filly and forgot all about his nag and meeting back up with us.'

'That sure sounds like Mason, Delmer,' Caleb agreed as he looped a leg over his horse's head and slid to the ground. 'The kid ain't smart like us.'

Delmer shook his head and then placed a long thin cigar between his lips and struck a match against the porch upright, hard and fast. His narrowed eyes looked into the dark interior of the sheriff's office as he cupped the flickering flame between his hands. Denver sucked smoke and then shook the match and flicked it at the white sandy street.

Spike placed a hand on Delmer's shoulder.

'Quit fretting, Delmer. There ain't nothing to fret about. Mason's probably holed up in the hotel with a bargirl or a hangover,' he postulated.

Delmer pulled the cigar from his cracked lips and pointed it at his brother. Even the dust that covered his face could not hide the grim expression carved into it.

'You reckon, Spike?' he drawled ominously. 'Ain't you seen it yet? Ain't you seen what I seen as soon as we stepped down from our horses?'

Caleb stood beside Delmer. His brow was furrowed.

'Seen what?' he asked.

'Yeah, what are we supposed to have seen, Delmer?' Spike added. 'I see you and the horse and this damn office. There ain't nothing else.'

'Look,' Delmer snarled and then pointed at the boardwalk beneath their feet. The droplets of blood had dried long before their arrival but were still clearly visible. They did not know it but they were staring down at the evidence of their brother's lifeless body being carried from the buckskin into the sheriff's office.

Caleb rubbed his neck. Although he knew what he was looking at, he could not bring himself to acknowledge the fact that their younger brother had spilled so much of his blood. To do so was to accept that Mason had met his Maker.

'Can't you see the blood, boys?' Delmer growled angrily as he poked the cigar back into the corner of his mouth and stepped back toward the buckskin gelding. He stepped down on to the sand and paced to the horse's saddle.

Spike and Caleb trailed the elder. Their expressions altered when they saw what Delmer was staring at.

'Is that blood?' Spike stammered.

Delmer nodded. 'Sure looks like it.'

'Oh hell,' Caleb cursed and shook his head in utter disbelief and sorrow.

Delmer stared hard at the dried blood that stained the leather saddle. The streaks of dried gore ran down the fender and covered the stirrup. Delmer blew out a long line of smoke at the horrific scene and then looked at both his brothers.

'I got me a feeling it's belonging to young Mason,' he rasped before filling his lungs with the grey cigar smoke again.

Caleb and Spike moved quickly to the side of their sibling and tried to think of another reason for the saddle being stained with so much dried blood. No matter how hard they strained their brains, the only answer that made any sense to them was that Delmer was right. It was Mason's blood.

'You figure he's bin shot, Delmer?' Spike stammered.

The older of the Holt brothers chewed on his smouldering cigar and rested a hand on the saddle. His eyes darted at his two dust-caked siblings.

'Nope, I reckon he's dead,' Delmer snorted.

Caleb shook his head in disbelief. 'Mason can't be

dead, Delmer. He's way too damn young to be dead.'

'I wish you were right, Caleb,' Delmer grunted. 'But there ain't a critter crawling that's too young to die.'

Spike rested his hands on his holstered gun grips as he considered the notion. He glanced at both of his brothers in turn. Although in his guts he knew that Delmer was more than likely right. Fury swelled up inside him as he kicked the ground.

'Mason might have only bin wounded, Delmer,' he suggested.

'If Mason was only wounded why'd he ride up to the sheriff's office and trail blood in there?' Delmer reasoned as he inhaled deeply on his cigar and then pointed. 'If he was alive, he'd have ridden to the doctor's down the street.'

Caleb and Spike could both see the wooden shingle hanging a few doors from where they were standing. They returned their eyes to their brother and knew he was right.

'Where in tarnation is he?' Spike asked angrily. 'And how did he get himself killed?'

Delmer turned away from the gelding and stared at the townsfolk that were gathered all around them and then drew one of his six-guns. He waved the barrel of his .45 at the crowd and then cocked its hammer. The crowd went wide-eyed and deafeningly silent.

Delmer walked toward a group of at least a dozen men and women. He waved his deadly six-gun at them. His icy stare burned through the smoke of the cigar between his gritted teeth.

'Where's the youngster that belongs to that buckskin?' he shouted ominously at them. 'Heed this. I ain't in no mood to be joshed with. Answer me or I'll surely kill you.'

There was no doubting that Delmer Holt was serious about his threat. The crowd could see the grief in his dark eyes as he closed in on them.

After what seemed like an eternity an old lady raised her shaking hand and pointed to the far end of town. She cleared her throat and then ventured.

'They took him to the funeral parlour, mister,' she croaked nervously. 'The poor boy was shot to ribbons.'

A cold chill raced through all three of the brothers.

Delmer walked nearer the old woman. He nodded at her.

'How'd it happen?' he asked.

She shrugged. 'None of us know how or where it happened, sonny. All we know is that a tall, skinny varmint with long black hair brung that poor dead boy into town. He dragged the body into Sheriff Scott's office and then lit out.'

39

Delmer frowned and pulled the cigar from his mouth. There was something about the description of the man who had delivered Mason to the sheriff that seemed familiar.

'Did you happen to hear what this critter's name was?' he asked. He tapped the ash from the cigar before returning it to his mouth.

The old woman was thoughtful.

'I didn't hear his name but I've just recalled something about the ugly varmint. Something mighty strange.'

'What you remembered?' Spike asked.

'That galoot rode out of here alongside a young gal who was driving a stagecoach,' the old woman told the three outlaws. 'She was tiny but shameless. That gal didn't have nearly enough clothing to cover herself.'

Caleb walked to the side of Delmer.

'I seem to have heard of an ugly bounty hunter with long black hair, Delmer,' he said fearfully.

'Me too,' Spike nodded.

The brutal confirmation that their youngest sibling was indeed dead, but that he had also been riddled with bullets suddenly brought the true horror into focus for the hardened rustler. For years he had not given a second thought to any of their mortalities, but now the glaring truth cut into him like a sabre.

'A darn ugly bounty hunter with long black hair,' he repeated as he attempted to collect his thoughts.

'I never seen anyone look like him, mister,' the old lady piped up before turning away from the Holt brothers. 'He was like a monster. His face all covered in scars.'

Delmer released the hammer on his gun and holstered it as he continued to dwell on the horrific words. He swung on his heels and started down toward the undertakers.

'C'mon, boys,' he growled. He started walking with his brothers flanking his every step. 'I've heard all about a critter that fits that description but I never paid it no heed. I never believed that anyone like that could actually exist.'

'You've heard of somebody that actually fits that old lady's description, Delmer?' Spike shook his head. 'Folks like that just make things up.'

Delmer glanced at his brother. 'She might be old but she told us what she saw, Spike. Why would she invent the scars and long hair?'

The outlaws were silent as they continued through the shimmering haze to where they had been told their younger sibling had been taken. The three Holt brothers slowed their pace as they neared the imposing structure decorated in a similar fashion to all

41

places that dealt with death.

As they neared the funeral parlour, Delmer's progress was halted by Caleb's intervention as he stepped ahead of his elder and waved his hands at the brooding outlaw.

Both men glared into one another's eyes.

'Get out of my way, Caleb,' Delmer ordered.

Caleb pressed his hand against Delmer's shirt. 'I've heard them tall tales just like you have, Delmer. I never thought they could be true. Are you telling me that there is such a critter and it was him that cut down Mason?'

Delmer gave a slow silent nod.

Both Spike and Caleb looked at each other as they felt an icy chill sweep over them. Caleb moved closer to Delmer and leaned close.

'Who do you figure that ugly *hombre* was, Delmer?' Caleb asked fearfully. 'What they call him?'

Delmer brushed Caleb aside and stepped up on to the boardwalk. He grabbed the door handle and then looked back into Caleb and Spike's faces.

'If I'm right, it can only be one bastard,' he hissed and entered the gloomy undertakers. A sudden flash caught the brothers by surprise. They stopped and raised their hands to their eyes.

As their eyes recovered from the blinding light, they saw a photographer emerge from under a black cloth with a sickening smile on his face.

Delmer swallowed hard as his eyes focused in horror at what the photographer had been taking a picture of. They had seen it before, but this time it was personal.

A crude coffin, which looked as though it had been hastily put together from spare lumber, was propped up against a wall with young Mason's body inside it. His lifeless eyes had been forced open with undertaker's wax for the photograph.

Mason had been stripped to the waist to display the bullet holes in his torso. It was not something commonplace in the West and the undertaker knew that he and the photographer would make a lot of money.

Delmer held his distraught siblings at bay as he stared at the horrific sight. Then his eyes drifted to the undertaker who stood beside the coffin.

The smile evaporated from the face of the undertaker as he saw the fury burning in Delmer's eyes. The small man cleared his throat as his partner folded the tripod and carried the heavy camera out into the blazing sun.

'What you done to my brother?' Delmer asked as his shaking hand pointed at the coffin and its pitiful contents. 'He ain't no prize hog to take pictures of.'

Fred Foley suddenly realized that these were no

simple passers-by looking to order pictures of the outlaw. They were kinfolk of the deceased.

'Brother?' Foley croaked.

Delmer nodded. 'Yep, my kid brother.'

The undertaker raised his hands and held them before him as if in silent prayer. He tilted his head and desperately tried to calm the furious outlaws down.

'The sheriff gave me permission to record the fact that your brother was killed, gentlemen,' Foley said. 'You might say it's historical evidence.'

'Where is this sheriff of yours, amigo?' Delmer snorted as he stared blankly into the face of Foley and clenched his fists angrily. 'Where is he?'

Foley could feel the tension rising within the confines of his funeral parlour. He quickly lifted the wooden lid and placed it over the coffin.

'Sheriff Baker is across the street in the café,' he replied before turning to face them. 'It was his idea. He said he needed proof of your brother's sad demise.'

Delmer turned and moved to the window. He pulled one of the black drapes aside and stared across the street at the small café.

'Why'd he need proof?' he drawled.

'To recoup the bounty money he paid to the hombre that brought poor Mason here into town,'

Foley responded. 'You see, Diablo Creek ain't got a proper bank and he had to pay the reward money out of town funds.'

Delmer Holt inhaled deeply.

'C'mon, boys. Let's go have a confab with the sheriff.'

'What about this bastard, Delmer?' Spike pointed at the shaking undertaker. 'Are we gonna leave him here?'

'He won't talk,' Delmer said as he moved back toward the demure Foley. 'Will you?'

Foley shook from head to toe as Delmer bore down on him like a riled grizzly bear. 'I'll not say a word. I swear.'

Suddenly Delmer brought a clenched fist up. His knuckles connected with Foley's jaw. The sound of bone on bone filled the small parlour. The undertaker collapsed like a sack of potatoes at the rustler's feet.

Delmer stared down at the unconscious man and then turned on his boot leather and brushed passed his brothers. The outlaw did not slow his pace until he reached the hitching pole outside the funeral parlour.

Spike and Caleb rushed out into the sunshine as Delmer checked his guns. His unblinking eyes did not deviate from the café.

45

'What we gonna do, Delmer?' Caleb asked.

'We're gonna have us a talk with that star-packer, boys,' Delmer answered as he stepped down and started walking across the sun-baked sand.

'What about?' Spike questioned as he tried to keep up with his elder.

'I'm gonna find out exactly who killed Mason and the sheriff will then tell us which way him and that under-dressed filly went.' He snorted as he rested a hand on one of his gun grips.

FOUR

Sheriff Jeb Russell had no notion of what was happening in his sleepy little town as he quietly finished his morning breakfast. Nothing had happened in Diablo Creek since the infamous Iron Eyes had ridden in with the bullet-ridden body of Mason Holt draped over the saddle of his buckskin. The seasoned lawman had not expected the arrival of Holt's kinfolk to alter things. For one of the few times in his long uneventful career, Russell was wrong.

Utterly unaware of the danger that had arrived in his normally peaceful settlement, he had been seated with his back to the café window. He dabbed his mouth with a napkin and then pushed his empty plate away as he finished his coffee.

Russell pulled a few coins from his vest pocket as he had done countless times before and placed them beside his empty cup.

He had only just risen to his feet when the Holt boys entered the café. The door hit the wall hard as Delmer led his brothers into the confines of the eatery. As the startled sheriff turned to stare at the hostile faces, he suddenly felt his heart quicken.

'That's him, boys,' Delmer snarled as he saw the tin star pinned to Russell's shirtfront before lunging at the lawman.

The elderly lawman barely had time to focus when his bearded chin felt the impact of Delmer's fist. As the waitress screamed, the sheriff flew over the table and then crashed in a heap upon the floor.

Delmer tossed chairs aside and lunged at the dazed sheriff on the floor. Before Russell had time to gather his wits, Delmer dragged him up and then held him against the wall. He repeatedly used his superior strength to beat the lawman against the unyielding wall boards.

'So you're the star-packer who dished out the blood money for our dead brother, are you?' he growled. 'Now it's your turn. But we don't want money. We want vengeance. Savvy?'

The sheriff could not reply. He could neither hear nor understand what his attacker was screaming into his face. The constant pounding of his skull against the wall was like the pounding of

Apache war drums.

Delmer swung the lawman around as though he were nothing but a rag doll. He held Russell upright and then threw a sickening blow to the older man's belly. No mule had ever kicked harder. The sheriff fell forward as the outlaw sent a vicious uppercut to his chin.

Russell was knocked off his feet. He flew backwards and crashed through the window. A million fragments of splintered glass cascaded over the lawman as he hit the boardwalk and then cartwheeled into the sandy street.

As his brothers raced out through the open doorway, Delmer jumped through the large gap where the window had resided until a few moments earlier.

The rustler stared at the lawman's bleeding face and then levelled a boot into the lawman's ribs. Russell arched in agony as Delmer grabbed him by the bandanna and hoisted him off the sand.

'Are you starting to savvy that me and the boys are mighty upset by you paying that back-shooter, Sheriff?' Delmer shouted at the swollen face dangling by his bandanna from the rustler's grip. 'Are you?'

Russell was choking from the blood that filled his throat as Delmer savagely threw him at the shattered café façade. The sheriff hit the wall hard and then fell on to the broken window frame. Jagged pieces of glass and wood tore into Russell as he fell face-first on to the debris.

The dazed lawman pressed his hands against the boardwalk and pushed himself up. The pain of the skin-tearing glass that cut into his flesh seemed to wrestle the ancient lawman out of his bewilderment.

Russell stared through his swollen eyes at the outlaws who surrounded him. He slowly began to realize who these men were and why they were so intent on his destruction.

'You're the Holt brothers,' he gasped before rising on to his knees. 'I've seen your likenesses on Wanted posters.'

Caleb and Spike nodded in unison as Delmer moved closer to the bleeding victim of his venomous fury. 'So finally the penny's dropped, huh? Now you better get ready to die.'

'We gonna kill him?' Spike grinned eagerly.

'Let me gut the bastard, Delmer,' Caleb ventured, like a vulture too eager to wait for death to take its natural course, as he pulled a long stiletto from his waistband.

Delmer ignored his siblings and grabbed hold of Russell's shirt collar. He dragged the lawman off his knees and stared into the bloody features.

'Now listen up, Sheriff,' he drawled in a threatening tone as his grip tightened. 'We wanna know the name of that varmint who killed and brung Mason here. We also wanna know which way him and his lady friend went after you paid them their blood money. Savvy?'

Sheriff Russell gave a slight nod of his head.

'I savvy,' he groaned.

'Are you gonna talk?' Delmer squeezed.

For some reason that even the lawman could not fully understand he spat into Holt's face. Bloody spittle ran down Delmer's rugged features and dripped on to his shirtfront. The notorious rustler could no long control his anger and gave out a horrendous scream a fraction of a heartbeat before he pushed Russell backwards with all his might.

The sheriff hit the porch upright hard. His spine connected with the edge of the wooden pole and stopped Russell in his tracks.

Delmer bounded up to the winded lawman, clenched a fist and hit Russell in the belly again. The noise that escaped from the older man's twisted lips echoed around the street as the waitress inside the café screamed in horror.

Delmer pointed at Caleb.

'Kill that bitch, Caleb,' he snarled as his pressed a hand against the breathless lawman's chest and kept

51

him pinned against the upright. 'She's giving me a headache.'

Caleb touched the brim of his Stetson and then ran back into the café. Within seconds the screaming stopped. A smile etched the face of Delmer as Caleb walked back out of the café and into the blazing sunshine.

'That was fast,' Delmer noted.

'She had no place to run,' Caleb raised his trusty knife and then wiped the crimson blood off its honed blade on his sleeve. 'Let me show you how I done it. The sheriff is skinnier than she was but a gutting is a gutting.'

'Maybe in a while I'll let you loose on this critter, Caleb,' Delmer hissed like a sidewinder as he stared at the defiant lawman. 'If he keeps being ornery, that is.'

Russell felt Holt's fingers press into his shirt until they had a grip on his flesh. He winced and then was thrown away from the small café. His hip caught the edge of the hitching pole and sent him spiralling into the side of a water trough.

The veteran lawman was sprawled beside the wooden trough. Blood ran freely from his mouth as he stared into the sand between his legs. The spurs of his attackers filled his ears as they once again surrounded him.

'Why don't you just shoot me?' Russell asked through blood-stained teeth. 'Just put a gun to my head and pull its trigger.'

Delmer drew one of his guns and aimed at Russell's head.

'I'll grant your wish if you like, old timer,' he said coldly. 'Nothing would give me more pleasure than killing the critter who paid out the bounty on Mason's head.'

'I just paid out the reward money,' Russell sighed heavily as more blood trailed from his mouth. 'I had nothing to do with killing your brother, Holt.'

Delmer pushed the barrel closer to the sheriff.

'But you paid the critter who did kill him, Sheriff,' he snarled. 'That's almost as bad in my book.'

'Should I stomp him, Delmer?' Spike asked as he neared the exhausted lawman. 'I'd crush him until he was nothing but gravy.'

'Patience, Spike boy,' Delmer said as he eyed his brothers above the seated sheriff. 'There ain't no hurry. We got us all the time in the world.'

Suddenly the eldest of the Holt clan jerked his wrist forward and slammed the barrel of his .45 into the temple of their helpless victim.

Russell saw a white flash as he rocked on his backside. His watery eyes stared up at Delmer.

'I give up, boy,' he said. 'You win.'

A devious smile crossed the face of the hardened outlaw as he stood above Russell. He leaned forward.

'What was the name of the bastard that killed Mason?' he shouted into the face of the defeated lawman. 'What was his name and which way did him and his fancy woman take when they left this town?'

The blistering sun burned into the bearded face of the elderly sheriff as he looked at the man he knew could end his misery by squeezing on his trigger.

'Why'd you wanna know, Holt?' he asked. 'Your brother's dead. Nothing can bring him back.'

A fury like nothing Delmer had ever felt before erupted in the guts of Holt. Even his watching brothers were shocked by the sudden explosion of their elder.

Like a rabid dog hell-bent on destruction, Delmer gripped Russell's bandanna and then lifted the lawman off the sand and dragged him back toward the trough. He powerfully dunked the old man's head into the water.

As Russell instinctively thrashed his arms around in a desperate bid to try and free himself from a watery grave, Delmer kept the battered and bruised lawman submerged. Bubbles rose around the head of the sheriff and slowly diminished in number until they stopped. Only then did Delmer haul his helpless victim out of the trough.

More dead than alive, Russell stared pitifully at the man who had his very existence in his grip. The weaker the lawman became, the broader Delmer's grin spread across his face.

'Not so feisty now, are you?' Holt taunted.

The ruthless outlaw released his grip and allowed the sheriff to slump beside the side of the trough as water continued to lash over him from the rim of the casket of water.

'You've beaten me, Holt,' Russell admitted as he sat limply at the feet of the hardened outlaw. He stared helplessly up at the three wanted men.

Delmer placed the barrel of his six-shooter against the temple of the lawman again. The cold steel braced the older man's attention.

'This is your last chance, old timer,' he said. 'I'm warning you. This time you answer me or I'll separate your damn head from your body.'

Russell nodded submissively.

'I savvy, boy.'

Delmer glanced triumphantly at his brothers and then returned his attention to the sheriff. He chuckled like a child who had just deceived his elders.

'Who was the varmint that killed our brother?' he snarled into the bleeding face of the man who was being held by his bandanna above the six-foot long trough. 'Answer me.'

Russell sat on the sand as blood and drool dripped from his mouth. He could feel the gun pressing into his skull. A cold shiver ran down his spine. He licked his lips and inhaled as best he could.

'OK. I'll talk,' the lawman managed to say through a deluge of blood as it trailed down his chin. 'Just don't hit me any more.'

Delmer straightened up but kept his deadly six-shooter aimed at the helpless Russell.

'Who killed Mason?' he yelled.

'Iron Eyes,' Russell stated as he rubbed his sleeve across his face. 'He said his name was Iron Eyes.'

For the first time since they had learned of their brother's death, they had a name for the man who had brought his carcass into town. The trouble was, they had all heard the name before. It was the name of the most feared bounty hunter in the West. A name feared by every man with a bounty on their head.

Delmer glanced at his brothers.

'It was Iron Eyes, boys.' he drily said.

A look of astonishment filled Spike's face.

'He's real?' he gasped in terror. 'I thought Iron Eyes was just a legend folks scared kids with.'

The sheriff glanced through swollen eyes at the confused outlaw and feebly pointed his bleeding hand.

'He's real enough, son,' Russell coughed. 'He's the most fearsome critter I ever seen in all my days. He looked like the Devil himself.'

'What was the name of the dame with him?' Caleb asked.

Russell shook his head. 'Damned if I know. She just said she was his woman. I didn't hanker to talk with either of them and that's why I paid the reward money even though I ain't meant to.'

Delmer pondered on the veteran lawman's words.

'Iron Eyes scared you so much you dished out the bounty on Mason's head?' Caleb queried naively. 'Does he look that bad?'

'Worse,' the sheriff answered. 'Nobody can imagine what it's like looking Iron Eyes in the face.'

Delmer toyed with his six-shooter as he listened.

Russell tilted his head back as blood ran from the corners of his mouth. 'There was no way that I was gonna argue with Iron Eyes, son. I feared that he'd kill me if he didn't get his blood money.'

Spike scratched his head, 'Are you serious?'

'Damn right, sonny,' Russell spat blood at the ground. 'He told me he wanted the money and I knew that if I didn't pay up, he'd just kill me too.'

'Holy cow,' Caleb looked to their elder brother. 'What the hell is this Iron Eyes critter, Delmer? He don't sound like no ordinary critter to me.'

Delmer rubbed his brow and studied the expression on the swollen features of the man at their feet. The sheriff was telling the truth and they all knew it.

'I don't care how ugly Iron Eyes is, boys,' he said. 'I'm gonna make him pay for killing Mason.'

The younger Holts moved closer to Delmer.

'You reckon that's wise?' Spike trembled.

'He sounds even worse than all them stories we've heard about him, Delmer,' Caleb added as he rubbed his neck. 'Mason was fast with his guns, but Iron Eyes must be a whole lot faster.'

'He must have tricked Mason,' Delmer stated. 'I bet this Iron Eyes shot Mason in the back or something. He couldn't have bested that kid in a fair fight.'

'We just seen Mason's body, Delmer,' Caleb noted. 'That boy was shot in the chest maybe a dozen times.'

'He must have tricked Mason somehow,' Delmer insisted.

Spike paced around the sheriff like a cougar watching its chosen prey. He had listened to all the talking and was none the wiser. All he knew for sure was that the infamous Iron Eyes was real and far more dangerous than he had ever imagined possible.

'Iron Eyes sure sounds like a real mean hombre, Delmer,' he reasoned nervously. 'I sure don't cotton to facing up to him.'

'He gunned down Mason for money, Spike,' Delmer said through gritted teeth. 'We gotta teach him a lesson.'

'Mason was a real fast gun,' Caleb added. 'If he couldn't better Iron Eyes, how can we?'

Delmer frowned in disappointment at his brothers. He shook his head and stared through the bright sunlight at them.'

'Are you scared?' he taunted.

'I ain't scared exactly, Delmer,' Spike shrugged.

'Me neither,' Caleb said cautiously. 'It's just we don't hanker after mixing it with Iron Eyes. That critter ain't like other folks. They reckon he can't be killed like normal folks.'

Delmer laughed out loud. 'Anyone can be killed. All you gotta do is get them in your gun sights and shoot.'

Russell looked up and warned. 'Don't bet on it, Holt. Boot Hill is littered with folks that figured Iron Eyes was a normal critter like themselves.'

'I ain't scared of anybody,' Delmer said out loud. 'I ain't never met a varmint that I couldn't better with my guns. I'm gonna get revenge for what he done to Mason. Are you coming with me?'

Both his brothers nodded.

Russell looked at the three rustlers.

'You'll end up like your kid brother if you ride

after Iron Eyes, boys,' he warned again. 'They say that he's already dead, but he don't know it. You can't kill something that's already dead.'

Delmer raised his six-shooter.

'Hush the hell up, old timer,' he snorted. 'Hush up or I'll surely kill you. There ain't no such animal as that. All men can die and Iron Eyes is just another man.'

'Do you reckon?' the elderly lawman ignored the warning of his brutal attacker and gazed through the blinding rays of the sun at Delmer Holt. 'I'm telling you that Iron Eyes ain't like any living man I've ever met before.'

'But he's still just a man, old timer,' Delmer spat angrily at the kneeling lawman. 'A whole heap uglier, but still a man and all men can be killed.'

'You don't wanna tackle Iron Eyes, boy,' Russell renewed his warning. 'That's plumb suicide. Listen to me. Iron Eyes just ain't human. He's a spectre. He's a living ghost that's too ornery to die and head back to Hell.'

Delmer stared down at the dishevelled sheriff.

'I'm starting to think that maybe I hit you too hard,' he growled. 'Your brains are rattled. Iron Eyes is just a damn ugly galoot, but that ain't no reason to be scared of the varmint.'

Russell glanced at Delmer's siblings. Unlike their

elder, they did not look quite so confident. 'Iron Eyes lives to kill and as long as you've bin branded an outlaw, that's exactly what he'll do. I've looked into his eyes, boys. It was like staring into the bowels of Hell itself. I'm telling you to forget about avenging your brother and ride in the opposite direction.'

A chill traced Delmer's spine as he listened to the bloody words that spluttered from Russell's mouth. Delmer dismissed his doubts and grabbed the lawman's head and turned it to face him.

'Which way did Iron Eyes and that stagecoach head?' he raged. 'Which way?'

Sheriff Russell pointed at the road beyond the livery stable and shrugged. 'The last time I saw them, they were headed thataway. That stage was drawn by a six-horse team so it should be easy to track.'

'The prairie lies in that direction, Delmer,' Caleb informed his brothers. 'Why'd they head there?'

'I heard that it's a death trap,' Spike stammered. 'Folks that head in there are never seen again.'

'I don't give a damn which way he went,' Delmer snorted at his nervous kin. 'If his tracks lead into the prairie, then that's where we go.'

Russell looked up at Delmer. 'Iron Eyes is mean. Pure evil flows in his veins.'

'Iron Eyes might be evil but so am I, old timer,' he grunted. 'He's just uglier than me.'

61

'At least you got that right, sonny,' the sheriff coughed.

Then without warning Delmer squeezed his trigger. A plume of smoke and a deafening flash of deadly venom spewed from the barrel of his .45. Within a heartbeat the skull of the lawman exploded into sickening gore. Russell was knocked backward by the impact and landed beside the trough. As the lawman lay lifelessly on the white sand, a pool of crimson spread out from his shattered skull and encircled his body.

Taken by surprise, both brothers moved closer to their older sibling. They looked down at the body and then at the smirking Delmer.

'What you wanna do that for, Delmer?' Spike frantically asked his unconcerned brother. 'That old critter couldn't have caused us any trouble. You busted him up good.'

'You killed him,' Caleb gasped in shock. 'Why?'

Delmer holstered his smoking gun and turned to face his younger brothers. Neither had ever seen Delmer look quite as evil before. There was a darkness in him now that they did not recognize.

'Why did I kill that critter?' Delmer repeated their question. 'I killed him because he paid Iron Eyes for killing Mason. That's why.'

'But he was helpless,' Spike shrugged.

Delmer stared hard into their eyes.

'So was that waitress in the café,' he spat. 'You stuck her with that long knife of yours just for screaming.'

Caleb shook his head. 'But you told me to do that.'

'Exactly,' Delmer grinned. 'Killing is killing. There ain't nothing to get fretful about. We're wanted and there are a lot of folks willing to kill us for the reward money. The trick is to kill them first.'

Spike raised his eyebrows and shrugged. 'What we gonna do now?'

'We fill our bellies with whiskey and then head on out after Iron Eyes,' Delmer said bluntly.

Both men turned toward the saloon as Delmer stepped over what was left of Russell. As he walked, smoke trailed from his holstered gun.

'Remember, I'm just as bad as Iron Eyes is, boys,' he smirked. 'Damned if I know what a spectre is, but whatever it is, I'm gonna kill it just like I killed that old sheriff back there.'

The three outlaws headed back to where they had left their horses tethered outside the sheriff's office. The saloon stood two doors beyond their steaming mounts.

As they got within spitting distance of the smell of stale tobacco and spilled alcohol, Delmer looked back at his brothers.

63

'I'm gonna teach that stinking bounty hunter that it don't pay to kill a Holt, boys.' He snarled. 'Iron Eyes killed Mason for money. I'm gonna kill him for free.'

FIVE

Squirrel Sally had driven her six-horse team for hours through the darkness toward the distant light before her keen eyes spotted an outcrop of massive smooth boulders projecting from the sand. With the expertise of a teamster, she managed to steer her stagecoach through a narrow gap between the rocks until its length was hidden from prying eyes.

After Sally had watered and fed her horses, she walked barefoot across the top of the coach with her Winchester in her hands and studied the unfamiliar terrain. There was little to see in the eerie light of thousands of stars. Everything had been painted with a coat of black and that suited the normally confident female.

Sally was comforted by the fact that if she could not see the warriors who had unleashed their arrows at her, then they could not see either her or the lengthy vehicle.

Once she had been satisfied that the only way that anyone could follow her into the narrow confines of the rocky hiding place was from behind the tail of the palomino stallion secured to the stagecoach tailgate, she relaxed.

After checking on her still sleeping passenger, Sally had climbed back up on to the roof of the stage and huddled beneath a spare horse blanket with her trusty Winchester in her hands.

She had not intended to sleep but that was exactly what she had done. After hours of unrelenting labour, Sally had slept as she had never done before. Exhaustion had over-ruled all other intensions to remain alert in protection of her beloved cargo.

The sudden shock of awakening in the bright sunlight caused Sally to throw the blanket aside as she got back to her knees with the rifle still in her hands. She shook her golden hair and then rubbed the sleep from her eyes.

It took several moments for the fiery young girl to fully realize where she was and why she was on top of the stagecoach roof. As her mind cleared, she looked around her. The smooth boulders towered over the long vehicle. They seemed much larger than they had when she had perfectly navigated her horses into the narrow gap between them.

Sally looked up. Although the desert was bright, she could still not see the sun from within the confines of the high rocks. That told her that it was still not noon. She got to her feet and walked to the edge of the baggage railings and looked down. There was barely twelve inches between the smooth rocks and the side of the coach.

'Phew,' she gasped and then proceeded to the driver's side and again stared down. 'That was sure good driving. Reckon I can handle this rig better when I can't see than when I can.'

Sally walked toward the rear of the vehicle. Her blue eyes narrowed and gazed out at the ocean of white sand. She bit her lower lip nervously as she pondered on the unseen Indians who had peppered her prized stagecoach with their arrows.

Her eyes looked down over the canvas-covered boot and then her heart quickened. Iron Eyes' handsome palomino stallion was gone.

Sally felt sick.

'Oh hell,' she cursed before asking herself. 'Where in tarnation has his horse gone? It was there tied up to the tailgate before I hunkered down for the night.'

The agile female held her rifle above her head and then slid down the canvas. She landed on the sand and checked the tailgate. The horse's long leathers had not been cut, she reasoned. The secure knotted reins had been untied.

'It's a good job that ornery scarecrow is asleep,' Sally said. 'He'd be mighty sore if he knew his pretty nag had been stolen.'

A host of thoughts filled her mind as Sally tried to regain her composure and figure out what she ought to do. She twisted on her bare feet and looked out at the white dunes which surrounded the massive rocks. Then she swung back and stared at the sand.

Suddenly, she spotted something which did not add up in her youthful mind. Her eyebrows rose until they vanished under her golden curls. Sally dropped on to one knee and called upon her unequalled hunting skills to read the situation and tell what had happened.

The harder she stared at the marks in the soft sand behind the large wheel of the stationary stagecoach, the clearer it became. Sally began to nod. Slowly at first and then faster as her agile brain figured it out.

It did not take the feisty girl long to work out exactly what had occurred at the back of her arrow-peppered stagecoach.

Her expression altered from one of concern to one of furious anger. Sally shook her mane of wavy hair in utter disbelief that it seemed her beloved Iron Eyes had once again fled like a jack-rabbit from her.

The deep tracks in the sand told her that Iron Eyes had walked from the coach and released his palomino from where his young companion had tethered it. It was a tight gap between the massive rocks and the stagecoach but the infamous bounty hunter was easily skinny enough to achieve it.

Sally squinted at the sand and muttered angrily.

She could tell that the bounty hunter had then mounted his trusty horse and ridden away. She ran along the narrow gorge and into the blistering sunshine. The sand beneath the merciless rays of the fiery orb was baking hot.

Sally retraced her steps back to where the sand was cooler and stared at the hoof tracks, which headed across a dune before disappearing from view.

She slid the barrel of her rifle through the rope cord holding her britches up and shook her fists at the blue cloudless sky.

Then her face screwed up as she glared at the stagecoach again. Sally knew that she might be wrong and someone else could have stolen the palomino, but the faster her heart pounded inside what was left of her tattered shirt, she doubted it.

Sally marched back toward the stationary vehicle and struggled passed its large rear wheel. Sally had to suck in her trim belly in order to achieve this and was only able to breathe normally once she had cleared it. Then as she went to reach up to grab the carriage door handle she heard the sound of cloth tearing.

Her eyes stared at her shirt.

Most of it was hanging on the metal wheel rim where it had become snagged. A rage exploded inside the half-naked female as she pulled the door open.

Just as the tracks had already told her, Iron Eyes was gone. She shook her head in a mixture of relief that her beloved man was well again and fury that for some reason, he had deserted her without explana-tion.

'You skinny swine,' Sally grunted as she hauled herself off the sand and squeezed her sweat-covered torso into the body of the coach. She plonked down on one of the seats and stared at the opposite bench. 'One minute you're looking worse than a dead skunk and smelling even worser, and then you sneak out and high tail it.'

She looked down at her well-developed bosom and shook her head as she lifted the cushioned seat and pulled out a new shirt. As she dressed, she mumbled at her absent companion.

'Why do you keep running off like this?' she questioned as she strained to pull both sides of the shirt together over her heaving breasts. 'I ain't exactly ugly. Not ugly like you are anyway. I got all the things that proves I'm a woman. I got me pretty hair and big chests.'

She managed to do up most of her shirt's buttons when two went flying across the interior of the stagecoach hitting the opposite wall.

'Damn it all,' she cursed again.

'I know what it is,' Sally said as she wriggled out through the stagecoach door and started to climb upward. 'It's coz I shot you, ain't it? You ain't never forgive me for shooting you when we first met.'

Sally crawled to the front of the vehicle and swung her hips over the baggage rails. Her rump landed on the well-sprung board as she gathered her long reins together and released the brake.

'Shoot someone once and they hold it against you for the longest time,' Sally sighed before pulling her Winchester free of her rope belt and placing it beside her.

With the confidence few ever attain, Sally expertly got her team to slowly back up. The stagecoach began to inch its way out of the rocky gorge toward the white dunes.

She poked her pipe into the corner of her mouth and chewed on its stem as she carefully guided the lengthy vehicle back to where she could turn it to follow the man she truly believed she was betrothed to.

The vicious sun started to gradually spread across the stagecoach roof as it emerged from the gorge. Sally slowly eased the long leathers to her right. The vehicle began to turn as its perky driver carefully steered it out on to the hot sand.

Her foot pressed down on the brake pole as she got her team in line. She then released the brake and got the six black horses moving forward.

'When I catch up with your sorrowful hide I'm gonna shoot you again, Iron Eyes,' Sally chuckled as her teeth gripped her pipe. 'And I ain't gonna tell you where I hid your bounty money either. I'll teach you to run away from me after I tried to save your damn life. Some critters are never grateful.'

The stagecoach moved between the dunes as Sally kept a watchful eye on the hoof tracks left by the powerful palomino stallion.

As the horses increased their pace, the hairs on the nape of her neck started to tingle. Sally squinted against the blinding sun as she looked around her.

Then she saw it.

From somewhere off in the distance Sally caught

sight of the one thing that reminded her that she was not alone in the arid desert.

Smoke signals rose into the blue heavens.

'Damn,' Sally gulped before lashing the reins. 'I'd plumb forgotten about them varmints.'

SIX

The white plumes of smoke rose up from the scarlet mesas as the bounty hunter slowed his golden mount and then stopped the snorting animal. Iron Eyes pushed his tangled mane of black hair off his face and stared at the series of white smoke. He gritted his teeth and continued to watch them as his hand fumbled in his inside pocket. His bony hand withdrew a long thin cigar and placed it between his razor-sharp teeth. He bit the tip off the cigar and then spat it at the sand.

There was a blank look carved into his mutilated face as he struck a match with his thumbnail and lifted it to the cigar. He filled his lungs with its acrid smoke and then tossed the match over his shoulder.

'How in tarnation did Squirrel manage to get us here?' he wondered before pulling the cigar from his mouth and exhaling a line of smoke into the air. 'That little gal sure dropped us into a mess of trouble and no mistake.'

His haunting eyes looked all around him and then he dragged his reins hard to his left and spurred. The magnificent horse galloped up a steep dune and then felt its reins being hauled back. The stallion stopped as its infamous master sat motionless upon the ornate Mexican saddle.

The bounty hunter might have been a statue. The only movement was the smoke that drifted from his gritted teeth as his eyes darted around the desolate ocean of sand.

Every fibre in his emaciated body told him that there were Indians somewhere in the desert. Yet no matter how hard his eyes strained, he could not see any of them.

Iron Eyes raised a hand and pulled the cigar from his mouth and considered the position he had found himself in. He had never travelled a land like this before. It was unlike anything he had ever seen before.

His hooded eyes darted to where he could see the signal smoke drifting up through the blue sky. A cold shiver traced down his backbone as his skeletal hand checked the savage wound that had caused him to lose so much blood and to sleep for over a day as his body fought to recover.

He was as weak as a kitten and knew it.

There was something very strange about this place, he thought as he rested on his magnificent saddle. This was not a place he would have knowingly entered as Squirrel Sally had.

His long bony fingers pulled his trail coat away from his blood-stained flesh as he studied the wound through the massive tear in his shirt. It had stopped bleeding by itself, which confused him.

Maybe he had run out of blood.

Iron Eyes thought about the smoke. Normally he could read signal smoke but he did not recognize the pattern of the large white plumes as they rose heavenward.

'Must be a tribe I ain't ever run into before,' he said as his thin left arm reached back and dragged out one of the whiskey bottles he had stolen from Sally's stagecoach earlier that morning. As he pulled the cork and lifted the clear glass vessel to his scarred lips, he wondered who these unseen Indians were.

It could not be Apaches, he thought as the fiery liquor burned a path down his throat. He had encountered most of the various Apache tribes over the years. They would never waste time making smoke when they could be firing their rifles and bows at him.

Most Apaches would attack their prey and overwhelm them with arrows and bullets. They would never hide from view. He scratched his hairless chin thoughtfully.

'Who the hell are they?' he rasped before lifting the bottle to his lips again and taking a long swallow. The whiskey warmed his innards as its fumes cleared his still throbbing mind.

Iron Eyes had never shied away from battling any of the various Indians he had encountered, but it had always been a fair fight although not one he was ever happy entering into.

As far as he was concerned, killing anyone, especially Indians was not a profitable thing to do. Wanted outlaws with prices on their heads gave him a good return on the bullets he filled them with.

Killing anyone else was simply unprofitable.

Yet it seemed that so far every single time he had been faced with Indians, whatever tribe they belonged to, a raging battle had ensued.

He rested the bottle on the elaborate silver saddle horn and stared out at the dunes. He had never seen so much sand in one place before and that was beginning to trouble the ruthless bounty hunter.

Dunes that resembled giant ocean waves could allow an army battalion to hide behind them. He tossed the cigar at the sand and then took one final swig from the bottle before replacing its cork and returning it to the satchel behind his cantle.

Just as the emaciated bounty hunter dropped the whiskey bottle, he heard a sound off in the distance. Iron Eyes' senses were alerted. For the first time since regaining consciousness, he realized that there were others in this parched landscape apart from himself. The smoke signals were far off, but the sound was much closer.

Too close for comfort.

His bony fingers pushed his limp mane of black hair off his horrific face and tilted his head to listen more keenly. It might not have been obvious to most men who heard the faint throbbing noise, but Iron Eyes knew exactly what he was listening to.

During his eventful life, he had heard the noise many times in many different places. From dense forests to barren deserts. Iron Eyes noticed the ears of his high-shouldered palomino prick up as it too heard the sound.

The bounty hunter swallowed hard and held the stallion in check as it strained against its reins. He could hear the haunting warning that all tribes shared when they were preparing to strike. It was the distinctive beat of drums.

The skeletal horseman knew that where there were drums, there were usually a lot of pretty ornery

Indians. The thought did not sit well with the still-weary bounty hunter. Pain from the wound in his side still troubled him. He knew that he was in no condition to fight anyone, least of all Indians with a grievance.

Iron Eyes gathered up his reins and turned his mount full circle. As the muscular mount rotated on the soft sand, the bounty hunter's keen eyes vainly searched the mountains of sand for a mere glimpse of his tormentors.

Wherever the Indians were was a mystery to the gaunt horseman. Then he saw another smoke signal directly opposite the first.

Iron Eyes stood in his stirrups and balanced.

His eyes darted between the signals.

Although he was unable to read what the smoke was saying, he knew from experience that it must have something to do with his and Sally's intrusion into their land.

Ever since countless white settlers had started to swarm across the plains and one treaty after another had been broken, the scattered tribes had become justifiably hostile to anyone entering what territory they still regarded as their own.

The bounty hunter was about to spur and put distance between the ominous drums and his prized palomino when another thought dawned on him.

Iron Eyes recalled the small female he had left in the narrow rocky gorge. When he had sneaked out of the stagecoach and ridden away on his powerful horse, he had not realized that the land was infested with Indians.

Then he recalled brushing passed objects embedded in the side of the stagecoaches bodywork. He had not given them a second thought until now. Now he believed that they must have been arrows.

He sighed heavily and tapped his large razor sharp spurs into the flanks of the palomino. The animal started to walk as its master brooded on the fact that Sally might have been under attack whilst he had been unconscious.

'Maybe that was why she had driven her stage into that gorge,' Iron Eyes muttered to himself. 'She must have bin hiding from the Injuns.'

The notion gnawed at his guts.

'Squirrel might not have bin sleeping when I lit out,' he mused. 'The little critter might have bin wounded or even worse. She could have bin dead.'

Although he would never admit it to either the cantankerous Sally or even to himself, he cared for the feisty female who had dogged his trail for over a year. He had grown used to her and it troubled him that she might be in peril.

'Damn it.' Iron Eyes dragged his long leathers up

to his chest and halted the stallion. He then swung the horse around and looked at the deep impression his horse's hoofs had left in the otherwise virgin dunes.

His bony hands clutched his reins as he shook his head in a bid to clear his mind. The heartless spawn of Satan was not quite as heartless as most thought he was.

'That painful little Squirrel might be a burr in my rump, but I can't leave her to fend off a bunch of scalp-hunters on her lonesome,' he growled angrily as he steadied the horse beneath his saddle. 'Besides, with her mane of yellow hair, she's a mighty valuable thing in these parts and most Injuns wouldn't be able to resist getting their hands on her. She'd command a darn good price south of the border.'

Iron Eyes thrust his spurs hard into the flesh of the stallion and thundered down the sandy slope in a desperate attempt to reach Sally before his worst fears became a reality. With narrowed eyes and gritted teeth he ignored his own pain and drove the palomino on.

With every long stride of his horse, the sound of drums seemed to get louder.

SEVEN

The three horsemen had crossed the unmarked boundary into the devilish terrain hours earlier and steadfastly followed the deep wheel grooves that cut through the sand between the crimson rocks flanking them. The churned-up sand between the wheel marks were proof that they were on the right course and that was good enough for the wanted rustlers. Having obtained fresh mounts in Diablo Creek, the three Holt brothers had started hunting the legendary bounty hunter after they had filled their bellies with cheap whiskey.

The trail was an easy one to follow so that was what they did. They had heard the horrific tales about Iron Eyes, but did not realize that the prairie and desert beyond held far more danger than that posed by the bounty hunter.

Exactly like the naïve female before them, they were totally unaware of the fearsome reputation of the prairie they had willingly entered. The deep grooves that had cut a distinctive furrow in the sand that even the most inexperienced of riders could follow lured the Holt brothers like flies to an outhouse.

Countless painted warriors moved like fearless mountain goats across the treacherous red rocks above them, noting every stride of their mounts as they moved through the sagebrush in pursuit of their goal.

Delmer led from the front as was his habit. His siblings dutifully followed as he rode deeper and deeper into the uncharted prairie between the scarlet mesas. Had they paused for a moment and allowed the echoing of their horses hoofs to fade, they might have heard the chilling drums that greeted the arrival of so many uninvited intruders into the hostile terrain.

Spurred on by bellies full of Diablo Creek's best hard liquor and a sense of revenge that defied every scrap of common sense they had once prided themselves with, the drunken outlaws headed on into the scarlet-flanked desert canyon. The three horsemen had only one collective thought between them. They had vowed that they would catch up with the notorious Iron Eyes and kill him for filling their kid brother full of lead.

Their fresh mounts had made good time since they had unwittingly entered the unknown land of jagged spires and unearthly mountain peaks.

Delmer Holt disregarded his brothers' protests.

He had already savoured the taste of blood and wanted more. He had killed his share of unwitting folks during his years as a cattle and horse rustler, but killing the elderly lawman had been different.

A sense of power had washed over him.

As he kept spurring his mount on into the parched and perilous land, he started to think that nothing could stop him from achieving his goal.

Delmer regarded Iron Eyes as already dead. He had marked the infamous bounty hunter for slaughter and in his depraved mind that could be the only conclusion.

Like so many others before him, Delmer considered Iron Eyes to be the same as all the other bounty hunters who roamed the West in search of men who, like his brothers and himself, were wanted dead or alive.

Nothing could have been further from the truth.

Iron Eyes was unlike any of the men who shared his lethal profession. The gaunt horseman shared little with other men and so far had proven impossible to kill.

Perhaps the stories about the skeletal creature were all true and he was, as the Apaches had branded him, a dead man too stubborn to return to the bowels of Hell. Whatever the truth might have been, Iron Eyes was indeed a far more dangerous adversary than the eldest of the Holt brothers had ever imagined.

Mason Holt had discovered that fact to his cost.

Clouds of blood-coloured dust rose up from the hoofs of their three mounts as the Holt brothers whipped their reins across the animals' shoulders.

Delmer leaned back against his saddle cantle as his lathered-up horse strode through the arid terrain and further into the prairie.

Had he or either of his brothers cast their attention up at the rocks that towered over them, they might have caught a glimpse of the strange unknown Indians who observed their every move.

'How far have we gotta go before we find him, Delmer?' Spike asked as he drew level with his obsessed sibling and mopped his sweat-soaked face with the tails of his bandanna. 'My rump is getting mighty sore trailing these stagecoach tracks.'

'Quit beefing, Spike,' Delmer grunted across the distance between them as the sickening heat haze grew thicker. 'By my reckoning that big old buggy couldn't have gotten far.'

Spike frowned as he stared across at his elder.

'And how do you figure that exactly?' he snorted. 'Wishful thinking?'

Delmer glared at Spike. 'We're catching up with that big heavy stagecoach with every stride of our fresh horses. A team of stage nags have to be watered and fed a lot more often than saddle horses do. We're gaining on them, boy. Pretty soon I'll have Iron Eyes in my gun sights.'

Caleb suddenly drew level with his brothers and frantically caught their attention. He was pointing up at the surrounding hills as his words fought to escape his mouth.

Delmer looked at Caleb curiously.

'What in tarnation is eating at you, Caleb?' he asked through a mocking grin. 'You look as sick as hound dog after a night locked in a butcher's store.'

Finally Caleb managed to speak.

'Injuns, Delmer,' he gasped and pointed up at the rocks to both sides of them. 'Look up at them rocks. There's scores of the critters.'

Delmer's expression altered as his whiskey-sodden brain absorbed his brother's words. The wide grin turned into a troubled frown as his narrowed eyes looked to where Caleb was pointing.

For a few moments he thought that the heat had gotten to his younger brother and he was seeing things. Then he too saw them perched upon their perilous vantage points along the crimson-coloured rocks.

Spike shielded his eyes against the glaring sun reflecting off the rocks.

'I don't see nothing,' he stated.

Delmer turned on his saddle and focused on the opposite wall of jagged peaks and then swallowed hard as his gloved hands gripped his reins tightly.

'Can't you see them Injuns, Spike?' he snarled as his mind searched for his next course of action. 'Damn it. They're on both sides of this damn canyon, boy. Can't you see them?'

Spike screwed up his eyes and strained. 'All I can see is this damn heat haze, Delmer. Are you sure there's Injuns up there?'

'Yep, I'm sure,' Delmer replied as he glanced all around them. Suddenly the prairie vegetation became more ominous as his imagination wondered what might be hidden behind the Joshua trees and cactus littering the baking sand. 'We're surrounded by Injuns.'

Caleb drew his horse closer as all three maintained a steady pace. He grabbed hold of Delmer's loose leathers to get his attention. He stared at his brother.

'What we gonna do?' his voice cracked.

Delmer pulled the brim of his hat down to shield his eyes and then looked straight ahead at the moving air that tormented him.

'We keep riding,' he snapped.

'But what if them critters decide to attack us, Delmer?' Spike nervously asked. 'With them to both sides of us, it would be a turkey shoot. We ain't got a chance.'

Delmer had never cared for pessimism and reached across the distance between them. He slapped his junior with the back of his gloved hand. It was something he had done countless times before.

'Hush the hell up,' he said. 'I don't care for that kinda talk. Always remember that we're Holts.'

Spike steered his horse just far enough away from Delmer before adding, 'Mason was a Holt, Delmer. A damn name don't make us invincible and you know it.'

'Maybe they're friendly,' Caleb suggested.

A stony silence filled the prairie air as Delmer looked up at the countless Indian braves dotted along the high ledges, their bows glinting in the brilliant sunshine. He snorted and jerked his leathers against his horse's neck.

'We keep riding,' Delmer insisted.

Spike was just about to protest about the wisdom of them trailing the famed Iron Eyes into the mysterious prairie when his attention was drawn to an unfamiliar sound to his right. The rider went to turn when he felt and heard a sudden thud against his thigh.

The outlaw thought that he had been targeted by a well-placed rock at first. Then a burning sensation rippled from where he had felt the impact of the blow. It was unlike anything he had ever felt before.

Spike's eyes darted to the growing pain in his leg and then saw an arrow embedded in his thigh up to its feathered flights. Blood seeped from the hilt of the arrow as the horrified horseman stared at it in disbelief. His right hand instinctively reached down to touch it. As his fingers reached the feathered flight an agonizing pain burned like a dozen red-hot branding irons.

The rustler screamed like a stuck pig.

'I've bin hit, Delmer. I got me an arrow in my leg.'

'So much for them being friendly Injuns, Caleb,' Delmer snapped at his other sibling. He stood in his stirrups but could not see the arrow in Spike's leg. He lowered himself back on to his sweat-soaked saddle and knew that there would be more arrows following the one that had already successfully found its target.

89

He signalled to Caleb and grabbed the bridle of Spike's trotting horse.

'Ride, Caleb,' he hysterically yelled out as he held on to his wounded brother's horse and then furiously spurred his own mount. 'Looks like them Injuns you spotted ain't partial to visitors.'

Caleb lashed the tail of his mount and raced off through a barrage of arrows that buzzed through the still prairie air in search of targets.

Delmer looked to both sides and saw the dozens of figures far above them amid the rocks. They fired their lethal arrows down at the intruders as the eldest of the notorious Holt brothers kept jabbing his blood-stained spurs into the flanks of his horse as he attempted to lead his wounded sibling's mount away from the unexpected attack.

As countless more arrows rained down from both sides of the towering rocks, the three outlaws rode into the swirling heat haze at break-neck speed. Dust drifted up from their mounts' hoofs as the Holt boys followed the tracks left by Squirrel Sally's stagecoach and horses at a feverish pace.

With arrows hitting the sand all around them, Delmer suddenly had a spine-chilling thought.

The hunters had suddenly become the hunted.

EIGHT

The high-shouldered palomino galloped through the blistering rays of the sun and rose up yet another steep dune. As the intrepid horse reached the top of the sandy rise, its master hauled back on his reins and abruptly stopped the animal in its tracks. Dust drifted from the stallion's hoofs as Iron Eyes stared through his narrowed eyes at the sight that unexpectedly greeted him.

His scarred features looked down into the gap between the dunes in disbelief. Every sinew of his emaciated form knew that something was wrong.

Very wrong.

His eyes studied the sight below his vantage point like an eagle studying its prey from a high thermal. Yet Iron Eyes was troubled. For the first time in his life he was concerned that leaving his precocious friend had been a mistake which might have proven fatal.

Iron Eyes thrust his spurs back into the animal's flesh and steered the palomino down to where the stagecoach rested amid disturbed sand.

As the stallion drew closer, the bounty hunter pulled one of his Navy Colts from his belt and cocked its hammer. As the long-legged horse walked toward the stagecoach, Iron Eyes began to fear the worst.

The six-horse team was gone from between the traces. All that remained were the wooden poles, leather straps and chains.

Iron Eyes glanced all around the area as his magnificent mount closed in on the stagecoach, but whoever had stolen Sally's black horses were long gone.

He drew back on his reins and dismounted swiftly. As his mule-eared boots hit the ground, a sense of total weariness washed over his tall, thin frame. He steadied himself against his handsome mount until his giddiness subsided and then inhaled deeply and continued toward the body of the coach.

For someone who had seen far more than his fair share of death, he was reluctant to look inside the stagecoach. A million thoughts flashed through mind.

What if the Indians who had taken the six black

horses had killed his Sally? The thought gnawed at his innards as he rested a bony hand on the coach door handle.

Iron Eyes knew that it took a special sort of person not to be afraid of someone who looked the way that he looked. To not only be unafraid but to actually seem to have feelings for him. He summoned every scrap of his inner strength and opened the door. He looked inside the stagecoach and sighed with relief.

Squirrel Sally was not lying there scalped as he had dreaded.

He lowered his head and composed himself. Then he turned slowly and studied the body of the coach. The bright sun made it clear that the stagecoach had been under constant attack by the number of arrows that were embedded in its bodywork.

His scrawny left hand ripped one of the closest arrows out of the stage and then he stared at it. His busted eyebrows rose because he did not recognize the feathered flight.

Whoever this tribe was, they were unknown to the bounty hunter. He then focused on the pointed tip. It was flint and that was rare nowadays since the arrival of a plentiful supply of metal due to the count-less white settlers who journeyed into the West.

Iron Eyes moved around the stagecoach.

As he reached the other door on the opposite side

of the stage, the beleaguered bounty hunter was convinced of at least one thing.

'This bunch of Injuns ain't got guns,' he surmised. 'They ain't got nothing like most tribes have collected over the years. No metal to forge arrowheads – that's why they're still using flint.'

Then he stepped closer to where the team of stout black horses had been taken. His eyes darted around the churned-up sand as he released his hammer and poked his Navy Colt back into his waistband.

'But they got ponies,' he muttered. 'A whole heap of them by the looks of it.'

The gnawing in his craw seemed no easier even though he was satisfied that Sally had not been slain. Something was still troubling the gaunt figure.

He turned and slowly walked back to the body of the stagecoach and opened its door again. He climbed in and stared at the dried blood that covered the padded seat that he had awoken upon hours earlier.

His hands searched the area within the coach.

He was looking for fresh blood. Blood that had not had time to dry. Sally's blood. There was nothing yet Iron Eyes was still troubled.

Iron Eyes clambered up the side of the coach until his painfully lean body reached the roof. He straightened up and walked to the driver's box.

Then his keen eyes spotted red drops on the long seat.

The bounty hunter stepped down on to the board and then dipped his fingers into the crimson gore. He lifted his fingers to his lips and dabbed the end of his tongue. He turned his head and spat.

'That's blood OK,' he sighed as his eyes surveyed the rest of the driver's box. He did not have to look far before he found a crude stone club lying deep inside the box. His bony hand lifted it and stared at the blood covered stone. 'By my reckoning Squirrel got her head hit by this weapon.'

He was about to discard the weapon when he noticed a few long hairs stuck to the sticky gore. They were golden hairs.

Iron Eyes felt guilty.

It was something he had never experienced before.

He knew that he should not have just left her the way he had done. If he had remained with her, things might have turned out differently.

His narrowed eyes then spotted something else. He knelt and reached down into the deep driver's box. His long fingers curled around the rifle and pulled it clear and rested it on the board he was sitting up.

'This rifle must have fallen down when she got

hit,' he muttered as he began to vividly imagine the events that had happened. 'Them Injuns didn't even know what it was. They couldn't have or they would have taken it.'

The words had only just left his scarred lips when he saw something else. It was Sally's corncob pipe. He picked it up and looked at it long and hard.

He threw the club at the ground and then slid the pipe into his deep trail coat pocket. His weariness had gone as Iron Eyes descended from the driver's seat and walked to where his sturdy stallion waited.

Iron Eyes was now driven by something he understood.

He slid Sally's Winchester under his saddle, picked up the reins and wrapped them around his wrist before stepping into the stirrup of his ornate saddle and mounting. His long thin right leg swung over the cantle and did not stop moving until it reached the other stirrup. Iron Eyes gathered up his long leathers and turned the powerful horse.

Iron Eyes needed fuel. He reached back and pulled out a fresh bottle of whiskey and pulled its cork with his razor-sharp teeth. He spat the cork at the sand and then started to drain the amber contents of the bottle.

The whiskey burned a trail down into his gullet and warmed his already fiery innards. As the fumes rekindled his hunting instincts, a wry smile etched his grotesque features.

'Don't you fret none, Squirrel gal,' he muttered before draining the bottle of its remaining contents. 'This bunch of varmints left me a good trail to follow. Just give them grief and I'll be there before they got time to spit.'

No sooner had the amber nectar reached his innards than the bounty hunter's honed instincts heard something to his left. A fraction of a heartbeat later, two arrows cut down through the smouldering heat narrowly missing his painfully thin body as they passed through his coat tails. Iron Eyes leapt like a puma from his horse, dragged both his Navy Colts from his belt, swung on his boot heels and blasted two shots in lethal reply. Muffled groans filled the air at top of the sand dune behind the stationary stage-coach. Two Indian warriors fell from their ponies and tumbled lifelessly down the sand.

They came to a halt at Iron Eyes' feet.

The gaunt hunter pulled his hammers back again with his thumbs as his piercing eyes studied the surrounding dunes for further braves. Only when he was convinced that they had been on their own did he release his gun hammers and ram both six-shooters into his belt.

'You boys shouldn't have tried to get the drop on

me with noisy horseflesh,' he drawled before mounting his palomino again and pulling a long black cigar from his pocket. He bit off its tip and gripped it between his teeth. 'Them nags up and killed you.'

He studied the bodies as he scratched a match across his silver saddle horn and cupped its flame. As he filled his lungs with smoke, his head began to shake back and forth.

They did not resemble any tribe he had ever encountered before. Their skin was stained with a red dye and they were adorned with silver trinkets.

'You sure ain't Apaches,' Iron Eyes mumbled through a cloud of cigar smoke. 'I can't figure out what you boys are 'coz you don't look like any Injuns I've ever bumped into before.'

His eyes read the hoof marks in the sand. He could understand what they told him, unlike the smoke signals that had earlier left him baffled.

Iron Eyes turned the palomino and spurred. As his horse thundered in pursuit of the Indians who had taken Sally and her team of prized horses, the infamous bounty hunter vowed that he would rescue the cantankerous female, whatever it might cost him.

With cigar smoke trailing over his shoulder, the bounty hunter shook his long black hair and stood in his stirrups. He had no idea how he was going to save Sally but he was going to try.

His mane of black hair bounced up and down on his wide shoulders as his horse gathered pace in response to its master's commands. Iron Eyes lashed his long leathers across the stallion's shoulders and followed the hoof tracks left by the unknown tribe. They would lead him straight to their stronghold, he told himself.

Then he would either save the feisty female or perish trying. It did not matter either way to the ghostly horseman, for death had been his constant companion for too many long bloody years.

Cutting a route straight through the sickening heat haze in pursuit of his prey, Iron Eyes resembled something more akin to the Grim Reaper than anything made of flesh and blood.

His matted mane resembled the flapping wings of some unearthly creature returning from the bowels of Hell to administer its own brand of bloody retribution.

The sun was on its inevitable descent.

The surrounding jagged peaks and gigantic mesas were reflecting their crimson glow across the desert sand dunes as day died and night was reborn.

The scarlet hue cast its unholy light across the determined bounty hunter as he whipped the high-shouldered palomino and forged on toward the unknown.

No spectral monster could equal Iron Eyes in full flight.

NINE

The trio of frantic horsemen had been riding for hours through the maze of prairie vegetation and on to the arid ocean of rolling waves; waves of white sun-bleached sand. The torrent of arrows that had rained down upon them had ceased, but the eldest of the rustling siblings had kept them moving until he felt sure that it was safe to stop.

As Delmer stopped his and Spike's mounts, his eyes searched the arid terrain like a fox searching for any sign of the pack of hounds he knew were still close. Delmer dismounted and moved around the nose of his exhausted mount until he was standing below his brother. Caleb rode back to his kinfolk and also dropped to the sand as he watched Delmer staring at the hideous blood-covered pants leg.

'Holy smoke, Delmer,' Caleb gushed nervously

before glancing at Spike's pale face as it drooped over his saddle horn. 'That ain't good. He's lost way too much blood.'

Delmer eyed Caleb. 'Water the horses. I'll tend to Spike.'

Caleb rubbed his unshaven jaw and obeyed.

Delmer raised his arms and placed his gloved hands around his wounded brother's waist. He carefully eased Spike off his saddle and lowered him to the ground. Spike was as limp as a dead man as his legs buckled under him and Delmer was forced to lower his brother on to the sand.

'You've lost too much blood, Spike boy,' Delmer growled as he rested on one knee and looked at the arrow. The gore-covered arrow tip had gone straight through his brother's thigh. 'Damn, this is bad.'

Spike's eyes fluttered as the words filtered into his dazed mind. He tilted his head and stared at his older brother and feebly forced a grin.

'Pull that sucker out, Delmer,' he said. 'It can't hurt any worse than it already does.'

The eldest of the Holt clan bit his lip and shook his head as his fingers checked the savage wound. 'I don't reckon that would be too smart, Spike.'

'Why not?' Spike asked as he fell back on to one elbow.

Delmer glanced around the desert, but all he

could see were the mountainous sand dunes that surrounded their resting spot and a sky that was slowly darkening. He returned his attention to his brother.

'If I do that, I might rip every vein left in your leg apart, Spike,' he muttered as he pulled out two cigars from his jacket pocket and placed them between his lips. He lit them both. He inhaled deeply and then transferred one of the cigars to his sibling's cracked lips. 'Suck on that.'

Spike barely had the strength to obey, but the taste of the smoke made him feel a little better.

'What you talking about, Delmer?' Spike asked through a cloud of smoke. 'You can't leave the damn thing in my leg.'

Delmer raised himself up on to his knees and unbuckled his belt. He pulled the inch-wide leather free of his belt loops and then wrapped it above the arrow where his brother's blood was still pumping in rhythm to his pounding heart. Delmer tightened the belt until its pressure forced the blood to stop squirting from around the wooden shaft.

Spike dragged feverishly on the cigar and then looked at his brother's bloody gloves. He watched as Delmer secured the strap and rubbed the blood down his jacket front.

'That's it?' he groaned. 'You gonna leave me like

this, Delmer? I can't spend the rest of my days hob-
bling around with a damn arrow sticking out of my
leg.'

Delmer stared at Spike and then looked over his
shoulder to Caleb. He whistled in the fashion most
men would use to attract a hound dog. Caleb reacted
in a similar way and walked the short distance to his
elder.

'What you want, Delmer?' he asked. 'I ain't
through watering these nags yet.'

Delmer held out his right hand.

'Gimme your knife,' he demanded.

Caleb pulled the blood-stained stiletto from its
sheath and placed its wooden grip on the palm of
Delmer's hand. He then shrugged and silently
returned to the horses.

Spike might have been short on energy, but his
instinct for self-preservation was still as honed as ever.
He raised himself up on his elbow and looked at
Delmer as his brother removed his gloves and ran his
thumb along the knife blade.

'What you figuring on doing, Delmer?' he asked
through cigar smoke. 'I ain't hankering to have you
cut my leg off.'

Delmer Holt looked up through his own cloud of
cigar smoke and then leaned toward his badly-
wounded brother. 'I ain't figuring on cutting your

damn leg off. I'm gonna try and cut the arrow out.'

Spike raised his eyebrows. 'Cut it out? That's sounds almost as bad to me. Do you know how to do that?'

Delmer stared at the bloody pants leg.

'It can't be that hard,' he reasoned. 'Like trimming a T-bone steak.'

'I ain't no T-bone, Delmer.' Spike vainly tried to scramble backwards, but Delmer rested his knee on his brother's boot leather.

'Don't move,' Delmer put the edge of the knife under the cuff of Spike's pants and then slid the knife upward. The bloody material split apart as the honed edge of the knife moved steadily past the knee and the horrific arrow protruding from either side of Spike's thigh.

Ash fell on to Spike's shirt front. 'You're starting to scare me, Delmer. What exactly are you doing?'

Delmer leaned over the arrow as blood trickled from the savage wound. He sighed and then pulled the cigar from his mouth and tossed it aside.

'This ought to work,' he muttered.

Spike stared at his concentrating sibling.

'Ought to work?' he repeated.

Delmer nodded. 'I reckon I've figured out the safest way to do this without you losing the rest of your blood, Spike boy. Relax.'

Spike swallowed hard. 'It ain't easy relaxing when you got that long knife in your hand. What are you figuring on doing, Delmer?'

Delmer pushed the brim of his Stetson off his brow and studied the arrow on both sides of his brother's thigh. He looked at Spike.

'I'm gonna cut the arrow shaft, Spike.' He explained calmly. 'Then I'll pull it through in the same direction that it was going when it hit you. It shouldn't bust any more of your veins.'

The expression on Spike's face matched his confusion. He leaned forward and stared at his brother. He poked a finger into Delmer's chest.

'Have you ever done this before?' he winced as the knife blade was placed on the shaft close to the feathered flight. 'I don't recall you ever doing this before.'

Delmer started to move the honed blade back and forth on the wooden shaft in a sawing action. 'Will you hush the hell up, Spike? This ain't easy.'

As the knife slowly progressed through the bloody wooden shaft, Spike screwed up his eyes in agony. He clenched both his fists and gritted his teeth.

'Sorry, Delmer,' Spike shook his head and drew hard on his cigar while pain rippled through his entire body. 'I'd hate for you to cut your finger.'

Suddenly the sound of war drums drifted through the dunes and caught the attention of the three

106

wanted rustlers. Caleb looked over his shoulder as his fingers carefully screwed the stopper back on his canteen.

'I'd hurry up if'n I was you. Delmer,' he advised as sweat trailed down his rugged features. 'Sounds like them Injuns have caught our scent again.'

TEN

The red rocks grew even larger as Iron Eyes thundered toward them. They loomed above the bounty hunter as he steered his palomino around the rolling dunes in pursuit of the Indians and their captive. His cold stare studied the countless hoof tracks that cut through the otherwise virginal sand and knew that they might be leading him into the jaws of Hell.

There were only two ways this could possibly end, he thought as he rammed his vicious spurs into the flanks of his intrepid stallion. Life and death were like a silver dollar being tossed up in the air for the ultimate of wagers. You had no way of knowing which way the coin might land and therefore you had to accept its random decision.

Some men hide when faced by danger. Others face up to the challenge and lay their lives on the line in the defence of those unable to defend themselves.

Iron Eyes had always chosen the latter course.

Even though he despised wasting valuable bullets on folks who did not have bounty money on their heads, Iron Eyes would willingly fight and kill anyone in order to save helpless females or children that were in danger and rescue them from the clutches of the real monstrous men who roamed the west.

His precious Squirrel Sally could never have been described as being helpless, but she had fallen victim to the overwhelming might of those who lived by a different code to the one which the bounty hunter lived by.

Iron Eyes dragged rein and stopped the snorting stallion.

As the powerful animal steadied itself at the base of a dune, the fearless bounty hunter listened to the sound that had tormented him for hours. The drumming was far louder now and he could hear the unmistakable noise of chanting as well.

Any normal man would have been frightened, but Iron Eyes was not like other men. He simply listened as his hunting brain formulated a plan which might or might not work.

All he wanted was to save Sally, but knew that he would have to kill a lot of her captors to do so. He gathered his long leathers in his bony hands and turned the tall animal so it faced the high scarlet-coloured rock face.

Iron Eyes leaned back against his silver saddle cantle and looked upward. The sky was no longer blue but changing as the sun began to set.

His narrowed eyes looked at the mountain in awe. He had never seen anything as large before and yet it did not deter him. A plan had started to ferment inside his head and he wondered if it might just work.

It was obvious that the Indians who had captured Sally and her six black coach horses had not imagined that they would be trailed back to their encampment. His searching eyes studied the high mesa which towered over the sand, but did not spot anyone upon the high craggy ledges. A wry smile etched his horrific features. There were no sentries upon the crimson cliffs, he noted.

'That's your second mistake,' he hissed ominously. 'The first was taking Squirrel.'

His bony hand slapped the cream coloured mane of his mount. The animal responded and powerfully rode up the dune and down the other side. As the sand levelled out, Iron Eyes closed the distance between himself and the foot of the blood-coloured rocks.

The haunting horseman glanced around the sand

as the stallion neared the immense monolith. There were no signs of anyone close to it. He looked to his left and stared at the sand dune that rested against the rock wall. The pulsating sound of drums filled the air.

Iron Eyes halted the stallion again. He balanced in his stirrups and looked even harder to where he could hear the continuous beating and then detected another noise.

The strange chanting and continuous drumbeats were louder now, he thought. So close he felt that he was within spitting distance of the warriors he knew were celebrating the capture of Sally.

Every fibre of his tortured being told him that the Indian encampment was somewhere beyond the hills of sand. He lowered his pitifully lean frame back down on to his saddle and looped his leathers around the ornate saddle horn.

Iron Eyes threw his right leg over the head of his mount and then slid silently to the ground. The sand muffled his mule-eared boots, but not his jangling spurs.

The bounty hunter knew that if he had been closer to the Indians, the spurs would have betrayed him. He leaned down and removed them from his boots before putting one into each of his deep coat pockets among the loose bullets he always carried.

Iron Eyes glanced upward at the darkening heavens, squinting and searching the vast sky and then nodded in satisfaction. There was no moon to warn his adversaries that he was bearing down upon them, he told himself. He looked around at the long black shadows which were getting larger in response to the fading light.

Iron Eyes silently vowed that he would use every one of the shadows to his advantage as he had done many times before in the past.

Squirrel Sally had no idea yet that her beloved betrothed was going to save her. Iron Eyes viewed the enveloping blackness and wondered if he might have bitten off more than he could chew this time.

He had no idea of how many Indians stood between him and Sally. He also had no notion of where she was or how to get to her without being peppered with arrows.

No matter how daunting the prospect of his failing was, he could not be deterred from doing what he knew he had to do. The skeletal figure checked the horse and then his weapons. He pulled spent bullets from both Navy Colts and then replaced them with fresh bullets from his deep pockets.

'I ain't gonna tether you, horse,' Iron Eyes told the palomino. 'If I don't come back, at least you can high-tail it before you starve to death.'

The gaunt bounty hunter moved to his saddle-bags, lifted one of its satchel flaps and looked in. He had two unopened bottles of whiskey left and knew that if things went wrong, he might not be able to replenish his stock.

His skeletal hand lifted one of the bottles, pulled its cork and then lifted it to his scarred lips and took a long determined swallow.

As the whiskey burned down into his guts, he patted the cork back into the bottle's neck and returned it to his saddle bag. His long legs paced back to the head of the horse and paused beside the animal's neck. Iron Eyes detached his saddle rope from his silver horn, looked upward and looped it over his shoulder.

The light was fading fast but that did not diminish the gravity of what he was going to attempt. The vivid red rocks were equally impressive in the darkness and probably a hundred times harder to scale.

Iron Eyes screwed up his eyes. He had spotted a ledge roughly twenty feet above him as he had ridden over the last dune – a ledge that appeared to go in the same direction from where he could hear the triumphant noises.

'All I gotta do is climb up there,' Iron Eyes whispered to himself. 'Find that ledge and then make my way along it until I'm right above the festivities. Then

113

I'll have to play it by ear, if I'm still alive.'

The scrawny bounty hunter moved to the rocks and raised his hands until he found a grip. He turned his head and stared at his prized palomino through his dangling black mane of hair.

'You'd better still be here when I get back, horse,' he growled at the handsome animal. 'If you ain't, I'll be mighty angry. Glue-making angry.'

With the determination and agility of a mountain goat, Iron Eyes hastily ascended the rocks. His height, light frame and long reach hastened his ascent up the rugged wall of rocks as he made his way toward the ledge.

A desert tarantula would have envied the speed that the bounty hunter achieved climbing up through the darkness as he reached the over-hanging ledge and gripped it with his long bony digits.

Iron Eyes mustered every scrap of his strength as he hung from the high rocks by one arm as his other hand desperately searched for something to grip. He swung back and forth until he was able to throw his right leg on to the ledge.

For a moment the exhausted figure panted like an ancient hound as he attempted to get his breath back. Then he summoned every last drop of his dwindling resolve and forced himself up and over the

114

crumbling rim.

His emaciated body scrambled on to the eighteen-inch wide ledge just as the last rays of the sun finally ebbed. Iron Eyes rested his back against the rocks and looked out at the desert sand below him. It was like looking at the sea as darkness swept across the rolling dunes.

He turned his head and screwed up his eyes.

The flickering flames of the Indians' campfire a few yards from the rocks drew his attention. A dozen high dunes separated the camp and his palomino. He could see their ponies and the six black stage-coach horses bathed in the dancing firelight twenty yards beyond.

Then he concentrated on the dancing braves moving hypnotically to the beat of the constant drums. His heart quickened its pace as he realized that from here on there was no turning back.

He could not get back down from the high ledge without breaking his neck. It was too dark to see any possible hand and foot holds. The bounty hunter would have to do what he had originally planned. He would have to continue on and hope that luck was on his side.

Iron Eyes carefully got to his feet and steadied himself on the narrow ledge before glancing away from his perilous perch at the barely recognizable desert below. The desert was bathed in a moonless darkness as a few final scarlet rays evaporated from the heavens. A million stars started to slowly appear in the black sky like diamonds.

Iron Eyes exhaled and rubbed the sweat off his mutilated face as his eyes looked at the narrow ledge. It had grown far darker than he had first imagined and it was virtually impossible to see it.

The gaunt bounty hunter adjusted the coiled rope over his wide shoulder and then began the dangerous walk along the ancient stony platform. Iron Eyes cautiously put one foot before the other and slowly started to inch his way toward the campfire light.

His narrowed eyes darted between his unsteady feet and the campfire, which he could see was being fed by the multitude of Indians.

The closer he got, the clearer it became.

Iron Eyes focused hard on the activities below him. There were far more Indians than he had even imagined possible in this arid region. His eyes darted from one group of warriors to the next as his mind attempted to calculate their number. Then he noticed that at least three quarters of the assembled Indians were females or youngsters of various ages.

He gritted his teeth thoughtfully. In all his days, Iron Eyes had never knowingly made war against womenfolk. His blood started to run cold.

Iron Eyes had never cared for wasting bullets on anyone who did not have reward money attached to their name. The law allowed outlaws to be legally tracked down and killed, but Indians were different. He would never waste ammunition on Indians if they did not start shooting at him first.

There was no profit in it.

Yet it seemed that from the Apache to the Cheyenne and a bunch of tribes in between, Indians just could not see the legendary Iron Eyes without trying to kill him.

He was like a red rag to a bull when it came to Indians.

Iron Eyes could count on one hand the warriors he had encountered who had not attempted to kill him. Mostly they saw him and reacted the way most folks react when they see vermin. They tried to kill him.

Maybe it was because they had built up a myth about the horrifically scarred bounty hunter. They believed he was an evil spirit that had to be destroyed. A spectre. They told tales about him which had grown out of all proportion concerning the ghost who could not be killed because he was already dead. So many colourful stories had been attached to Iron Eyes that he knew it was impossible to do anything but accept the fact that Indians genuinely believed them.

As his keen eyes studied the dancing braves he wondered if this unknown tribe would react in the same way that all of their brothers across the West acted.

Beads of sweat dripped from his long limp hair as he continued to move along the uneven and perilous pathway in the sky. He knew that if they caught sight of him, they would probably unleash their weaponry. He would be forced to start shooting and that troubled him.

'This is gonna get mighty messy,' he whispered under his breath as he peered down at the dancing figures around the fire. 'I sure hope I've got enough bullets.'

ELEVEN

Had the petite female been conscious when her captors brought her to their stronghold she might have seen the sheet of polished metal hanging from the rocks. It resembled a Spanish breastplate but none of the isolated Indians knew how or why it had been suspended above the mouth of the cave they still used in their ancient rituals. Its surface reflected the light of their torches and campfire out into the desert. This was what had lured Sally as she had desperately tried to find a safe haven in the arid desert.

But she had not seen it or anything else after being hit by a warrior's club. Now all she could do was fight to awaken from the perilous pit she helplessly found herself trapped within.

Countless demons taunted Squirrel Sally as she

struggled against her bonds and sank deeper into the bottomless pools of a place that she had never travelled to before. Monsters swept through her mind and disappeared before she could confront them. Sally tried to lash out with her fists, but for some unknown reason, she was unable to move. Black ravens swooped through the confused haze that was her mind and pecked at her. She could feel her flesh being ripped from her bones and then she heard the constant beat of pounding hearts. Then she saw the tall lean figure watching her from the distance. It was Iron Eyes, but he was just watching her with glowing red eyes that burned the air. She could feel the heat burning into her. Sweat trailed down her face and burned her eyes, but she was unable to look away.

Sally wanted to reach out to the haunting man as a mysterious breeze caught the tails of his ragged trail coat and lifted his long black hair. She stared at him but he did not move a muscle. He, like her, seemed unable to move.

She screamed out but there was no sound.

The only noise came from the constant throbbing of a heartbeat that grew and grew until it became unbearable. Sally twisted and fought against whatever it was that was restraining her, but it was useless.

A panic rippled through her young body unlike anything she had ever experienced before. Then she heard chanting all around her. She tried to run but her legs seemed helpless and nailed to the ground. Flashes of bright crimson and the blackest of blacks pulsated inside her mind.

Sally looked to where the statuesque figure had been watching her, but he was gone. Iron Eyes was gone. A chilling terror swept through her as she suddenly realized that she was alone. Her eyes opened and she bellowed.

'Iron Eyes,' she yelled out before it dawned on her that everything that had tormented her dazed mind had only been a feverish dream. Her eyes looked all around and slowly began to adjust to the reality, which was far more nightmarish than anything her delirium had manufactured.

It might have been the constant drumming or the guttural chants which had finally brought the golden-haired female out of her unconsciousness. Whatever it was, it seemed unreal to the logically-minded Sally.

The light of the Indian campfire danced across the rocks above her as countless warriors moved between the roaring flames and where she was restrained.

Sally tried to move but it was impossible. Somehow she had been tied down on a flat rock. Her dazed mind attempted to work out what had happened to her and how she had ended up here in the middle of an Indian camp. Yet no matter how hard she tried, she simply could not figure any of it out.

The last thing she could recall was sitting on her high driver's seat atop her stagecoach. She blinked hard and then realized that she was no longer whipping the backs of her team of black horses and thundering in pursuit of her beloved Iron Eyes.

The memory of the tall silent figure returned to her. Iron Eyes had only been part of the nightmarish vision which she had fought to escape.

She sighed dispiritedly. Where was Iron Eyes when she really needed him? The question burned like a branding iron in her young mind. Tears welled up in her beautiful eyes. Sally went to rub them away but her hands could not move. They were tied down to something she had yet to see or comprehend.

Just as in her nightmare, she was restrained.

Sally glanced at her left hand and saw the rawhide laces that had been lashed around her wrist. Blood trickled from the crude rawhide fastenings, showing that she had fought feverishly against her bonds while asleep. Slowly she began to become aware of what was happening and it troubled her. Sally had been in numerous scrapes since she had left home and decided to tag along with the fearsome bounty hunter, but nothing like this.

She blinked again but it did not stop the pain coming from the bruise on the back of her head hidden beneath her wild golden locks.

The dancing warriors, decorated in their feathered finery, drew her attention. They looked all fired up for something and she did not care to dwell on what that might be.

Her eyes slowly focused on the braves as they circled the campfire.

'This ain't good,' she whispered to herself.

They were Indians OK, but unlike any she had ever seen or heard of in her short but eventful life. The dancers wore full head masks made of clay and their bodies were also covered in it. They did not look remotely human as they chanted and moved in laboured actions.

The horde of other Indians who watched the dancers perform their ritual appeared more normal, but even they were clad in unfamiliar dress.

Sweat trailed down from under her blonde tresses as the severity of her situation became more and more apparent. Sally was in trouble.

Big trouble.

Every ounce of her tiny form wanted to run for cover. Sally went to do exactly that when she felt her restraints holding her on the smooth flat rock. She wrestled furiously but then realized that not only her arms were tied, but also her legs. Pain traced up from her ankles as the rawhide cut into her skin.

Sally lay on her back and cursed silently.

She was totally helpless.

Spread-eagled like a sacrificial offering.

Her blue eyes flashed from side to side in a vain search for a way out of her present troubles. No matter where she looked, all she could see were the strangely-decorated braves who surrounded her.

Her mind tried to work out what had happened.

How did she get from the stagecoach to this place?

Yet no matter how hard she tried to remember, all she could recall was waking up here.

'Where the hell am I?' Sally yelled.

To her utter surprise, her innocent question echoed all around her. She began to realize that she was in the mouth of a cave close to the desolate desert sands. Sally's eyes widened as she lay on her back straining at her shackles.

I gotta escape, she thought. But how?

The golden-haired youngster fought against her restraints until she was able to tuck her shoulder under her. Lying on her side, Sally stared out between the dancing warriors and caught sight of her team of six black horses. Behind the sturdy stage-coach team were countless painted ponies.

Thoughts of what these unknown people might do

124

to her haunted Sally. They did not seem to have any guns or any of the things other tribes had gradually adopted from the relentless settlers who continued to move through the west. No rifles or metal knife blades and arrowheads. Sally lay on her back and pondered that simple fact.

Who were they?

She had encountered several different tribes since she had started to travel with the gaunt bounty hunter yet they all appeared to be far more superior compared to these Indians.

Her headache began to ease in defiance of the throbbing beat of the drums her captors kept striking. Her dazed mind began to understand her surroundings better as several of the older Indians walked toward her and pushed her head back against the stone slab.

Sally gritted her teeth and frowned at them.

'You wouldn't be so damn rough if I had my rifle,' she snarled at them. 'I could kill a dozen of you varmints before I had to reload.'

Then Sally considered how many Indians there actually were and it dawned on her that ten fully-loaded Winchesters would not be enough. There were just too many of them and that simple fact clawed at her craw.

She shook her head and her wavy hair rested on the smooth surface of the rock. Several of the females moved closer to her and stared in admiration at the unusually coloured mane. They had never seen hair that colour before and it fascinated them. A large warrior with dark pigment painted across his face and down his torso ushered them away with a wave of a crude club.

Unknown to Sally, it was similar to the club which had been expertly thrown at her when she was driving her stagecoach. The solid stone ball had hit the back of her head and knocked her senseless.

Sally felt like a prize hog at an auction.

Whatever their intentions were, she knew that she would be kept in the dark until it suited her captors. She looked up at the rocks that hung over the flat stone that she was tethered upon. The light of the flames were catching the cave rocks which arched over where she was being held.

Sally closed her eyes and started to quietly pray.

She was not very good at it and had learned the little she knew from her late mother. After a few moments she opened her eyes again and stared over her half-exposed breasts to where the constant drumming was coming from.

Sally lifted her head and stared toward ten seated elderly warriors beating on petrified logs. The strain of looking along her spread-eagled body became too much for Sally and she was forced to rest her head

126

back down.

'Where the hell are you, Iron Eyes?' she muttered as dancing warriors started to close in on her. 'You ain't never around when a gal needs you.'

She blew some of her blonde strands of hair off her face in an attempt to see more, but it was useless. All she could see were the near-naked Indian braves who danced around her.

Sally tried to find strength to fight her bonds.

It was useless.

Sally was tired and had resigned herself to what she believed would prove inevitable. No matter how hard the feisty female tried to be positive, she knew that without her rifle or the help of her beloved Iron Eyes, she was doomed.

Sally had never felt fear before until this very moment and it weighed heavily on her petite form. Somehow this bunch of Indians had managed to get the better of her. They had done what she had thought impossible and transported her from her stagecoach to this place.

She had faced many daunting enemies alongside her beloved Iron Eyes, but she always had her trusty Winchester in her hands then and now she was utterly helpless. There was nothing to fend off the dancing and chanting men who had her at their mercy.

Whatever fate awaited her, it was their choice to dish out as they so desired. They held the power of life and death over her and Sally began to realize that.

A defiant smile came to her handsome features. Sally knew that she could either die crying or face it as Iron Eyes always did.

Head on.

'Don't you hombres know a different tune?' Sally shouted at them. 'That 'un is wearing mighty thin.'

If this was a game of stud poker, she told herself, the Indians held all the aces and picture cards. The deck was stacked against her.

All she had was a thin hope that a miracle might happen.

TWELVE

The sound of the drums had claimed another few victims with their relentless pounding. Each echoing beat sounded like nails being driven into their coffins. Delmer Holt had tended his wounded brother as best he could and then helped the weary rustler back on to his mount before throwing himself back on to his own saddle. Caleb had been nervously listening to the constant drumbeats as Delmer had finally removed the arrow shaft from Spike's leg and had mounted long before either of his infamous siblings had risen from the sand.

The trio of outlaws had kept on riding as the sun finally set and darkness had spread across the arid terrain. Delmer led the way between the sand dunes in a vain effort to find somewhere that might offer them sanctuary.

Yet no matter how far any of the three rode, they could not outrun the sound of the beating drums. The echoing noise of clubs striking drums seemed to be everywhere in the desert as the Holt brothers forged on.

Delmer had never been in a situation like this before. He was gradually becoming less and less confident that they would ever catch up with the infamous bounty hunter, let alone kill him.

The drumming grew louder the further into the desert they rode. The brothers were starting to tire of the chase and beginning to wonder if the Indians might be luring them into a trap. Delmer slowed his mount and glanced at Spike before turning his attention to Caleb.

'Spike's half dead, Caleb,' he muttered as he stared at the churned up sand before them. 'I'm starting to worry that he might have lost way too much blood before I dug that arrow out of him.'

Caleb looked grim as he anxiously looked around the starlit dunes. He nodded in agreement.

'We gotta get out of this damn desert while we still can, Delmer,' he said bluntly. 'Spike needs a doc to check out that wound. Besides, we're almost out of water.'

Delmer rubbed the sweat off his face as he glanced at the wheel grooves in the otherwise undisturbed

130

sand. He looked at Caleb and swallowed hard.

'There's gotta be a water hole out here someplace, Caleb boy,' Delmer said. 'That Iron Eyes and his lady friend wouldn't be heading this deep into the desert if they didn't know where to find water.'

'I ain't so sure, Delmer,' Caleb disagreed as he strained to see anything in the darkness that surrounded them. 'I got me a feeling that maybe they were carrying their own supply of water in that stage.'

Delmer's expression changed. 'I hadn't figured on that.'

Caleb rubbed his neck as he teased his trotting horse onward through the dunes. 'This desert is a lot bigger than I thought it was. By my reckoning if we turn back now we might just be able to get back to Diablo Creek.'

Delmer glanced back at Spike. It was clear that their brother was more dead than alive. He eased back on his reins and stopped his mount and then grabbed Spike's bridle and halted his mount as well. Caleb circled his brothers.

'We turning back, Delmer?' he asked.

Before the eldest of the Holt clan could reply, a flurry of arrows buzzed through the darkness over a dune to their right. The deadly projectiles hit the sand all around the three horsemen in quick succession.

131

Caleb hung on to his skittish mount as it reared up and kicked its hoofs at the haunting noise.

'It's them damn Injuns again, Delmer,' he screamed as he fought with his horse. 'They're still with us.'

'Damn it all,' Delmer snarled as he tried to figure out where their unseen attackers were. 'Where are they?'

The outlaw did not have to wonder for long. The words had barely left his lips when suddenly a dozen mounted braves came thundering over a dune behind them astride their painted ponies.

Caleb's jaw dropped as he hastily pointed at the warriors who were galloping straight at them. He had never seen anything like them. 'Look at them critters,' he screamed as total fear gripped him. 'Look at them, Delmer.'

The older Holt steadied his mount.

'I seen them,' Delmer shouted and then whipped the tail of Spike's mount sending the animal thundering ahead. 'You ride with Spike, Caleb. I'll try and fend them off.'

All three of the rustlers galloped between the high standing dunes. For a few moments it seemed that they had managed to leave their attackers eating their dust.

Then the truth dawned on them.

132

Whooping braves burst through the starlight in all their painted glory. Just the sight of the wailing braves was enough to put the fear of God into the brothers as they whipped and spurred their saddle horses in a vain attempt to outrun their pursuers. Yet unlike the trim Indian ponies, the outlaws' far larger mounts were laden down with weaponry and saddles. The Indians were soon breathing down the necks of their hapless prey.

Delmer cocked the hammer of one of his pistols, swung around on his saddle and fired a shot. He then straightened up as a flurry of arrows narrowly missed him and embedded into the sand beside him. As he kept encouraging his beleaguered mount on, Delmer looked over his shoulder again. The sight that greeted his sore eyes sent terror surging through his body.

'Holy Lucifer,' Delmer cursed frantically. 'What the hell have we ridden into?'

As Delmer chased his brothers up and over a dune, he felt a sudden chill as a flint axe hurtled within inches of his shoulder. His eyes widened as the animal beneath him galloped after his brothers. As his exhausted saddle horse reached the foot of the dune he heard the chilling sound of the charging Indians behind him.

Delmer twisted on his saddle and looked back to

the top of the sandy rise just as the small band of Indians cleared the dune and came charging down the churned-up sand. The warriors held their bows and hatchets in readiness as they chased the three outlaws deeper and deeper into the starlit desert.

The eldest of the Holt boys suddenly felt his heart pounding inside his shirt. He had never been so frightened in all his days. He fired his six-shooter at the warriors who were chasing them down.

Then he saw a few of the Indians prime their bow-strings with arrows and unleash their arrows.

Mingled with the sound of their horses desperately trying to escape their attackers, the desert hummed with the noise of arrows flying through the air.

It sounded like crazed hornets to the outlaws as Delmer allowed Caleb to lead the barely conscious Spike to safety and then fired his trusty Colt again. With arrows raining down upon them, Delmer blasted the last of his six-gun's bullets into the howling braves.

Two of the painted Indians toppled off the backs of their ponies and crashed into the shadows but the rest of them kept up their pursuit. The Indians spread out behind the terrified outlaws and unleashed more venomous fury.

Delmer holstered one gun and drew another.

There was hardly a pause in the outlaw's feverish

firing as he tried to kill the warriors before they killed him and his brothers. The desert lit up every time the eldest of the Holt clan fired his six-shooter but to the seasoned rustler's surprise, the Indians were not scared by the deadly shots.

They kept chasing and firing their arrows at the galloping outlaws. Delmer rammed his spurs into the flanks of his mount as his thumb pulled back on his gun hammer.

Shot after shot erupted from the seven-inch barrel at the charging Indians but they still kept chasing. Delmer could not understand why his smoking gun seemed unable to stop the Indians.

They were totally unafraid.

As his mount kept thundering through the starlit desert, Delmer glanced ahead at his brothers and then holstered his gun before leaning forward and dragging his Winchester from its saddle scabbard. He hauled the rifle up as he looked back at the charging warriors.

It was like looking at his own tombstone.

THIRTEEN

Iron Eyes rested on his knees as he studied the Indians below his high perch. He had noticed that they were sharing jugs of liquid and the more they drank, the more fevered they were becoming. The gaunt bounty hunter had heard tales of the effect some of the desert plants had when distilled like whiskey. They were said to have almost hypnotic qualities when consumed in large enough amounts. His narrowed eyes told him that the stories must be true as he observed many of the braves and females looking worse for wear.

Iron Eyes rubbed his scarred jawline thoughtfully.

Maybe he could use this to his advantage, he thought. Yet how could he do that? His remained crouched on the tiny ledge as his eyes darted all around him in search of inspiration.

Sally was definitely down there. He had heard her distinctive yells from halfway up the steep rock face. There was no mistaking her voice, especially when she was mad.

A smirk traced his brutalized face. He wondered how long the strange looking warriors would last if he did nothing and just left the fiery female where she was.

The Indians would not be dancing around the massive bonfire, he thought. The poor critters would be throwing themselves on to the flames.

Iron Eyes mopped the sweat off his brow on the back of his hand and then found what he had been searching for. A formation of rock that he could secure his rope to. He cautiously stood and then turned toward the rocks bathed in the blackest of shadows.

He removed the rope from his shoulder and uncoiled its lasso until it fitted over the craggy surface of the jagged rock. Then he tightened the loop and carefully turned back so that he was looking straight down at the campfire.

Iron Eyes sighed.

A hundred doubts flashed through his mind. He knew that to attempt climbing down to the ground would not work. By the time he got halfway down its length, he would be filled with arrows.

There had to be another choice.

He leaned against the rocks with the coiled rope in his bony hands. The only other option that he could think of was to throw himself off the ledge and swing into the mouth of the cave.

That would be fast and help him avoid being peppered with arrows as he descended, but once down on the sand, he would be at their mercy.

Iron Eyes only had twelve shots available to him before he would be forced to reload, his calculating mind reasoned. Iron Eyes was fast, but was he fast enough at reloading his prized guns? He sighed again.

'I need me a distraction,' he quietly muttered. 'But what kinda thing would get them Injuns looking in the wrong direction?'

It seemed hopeless, but the pitifully thin bounty hunter kept staring down like an avenging angel at the flames which licked the sky and sent scarlet orbs floating into the night air.

'Sure wish I had me a few sticks of dynamite,' he rasped as he held the rope firmly in his skeletal grip. 'That would sure scare them critters long enough for me to get to Squirrel and figure out how to get out of here.'

Iron Eyes shook his head.

'I need me a cigar,' he whispered angrily.

His bony fingers had only just dipped into one of his deep trail coat pockets when his busted eyebrows rose in sudden realization. Beneath the sharp spurs that he had pushed into the deep pocket earlier, Iron Eyes could also feel dozens of bullets milling around where he always kept them.

'I don't need dynamite,' he grinned. 'I got me a few dozen bullets in my pockets. Bullets explode just like dynamite does if you toss them into a hot enough fire.'

The ghostly eyes looked back at the massive campfire below his high perch. He started to nod to himself knowingly as he gripped a handful of bullets in hand.

'Reckon that fire is plenty hot enough,' he said coldly.

FOURTEEN

Delmer Holt cradled his Winchester as he thrust his spurs into the exhausted horse beneath him. Arrows flew across the head and neck of the animal as its master dragged on his reins and forced the horse between two mountains of sand. More lethal missiles flew into the ground ahead of the flagging outlaw. As his horse pounded beneath him he pushed the hand guard down and then pulled it back up. He swung around, levelled the rifle barrel at the Indians and fired.

The dunes to both sides of him lit up for a fraction of a heartbeat as a white-hot plume of deadly venom sped from the rifle barrel. Another of the Indians was punched from the back of his painted pony by the force of the bullet and sent crashing into the sand.

'I got me more bullets than you got braves,'

Delmer shouted at the remaining Indians and then rapidly cocked his weapon again. As the gunsmoke cleared, the smile faded from his hardened features.

To his surprise, the rest of the Indians were still chasing him and his brothers. The fact that he had already whittled them down did not seem to matter to the braves. It only fuelled their desire to get even with the uninvited horsemen who were trespassing on their land.

'Damn it all,' Delmer raged.

He cocked his rifle and fired again. The blinding flash from his Winchester came at the same time as the deafening sound echoed around the starlit dunes.

Then Delmer watched in horror as at least half the Indians primed their bows with more arrows. Terror ripped through the outlaw. He turned, gathered up his long leathers and whipped the tail of his flagging mount with his rifle barrel.

He did not have to see the warriors fire their arrows.

His ears heard them clear enough.

Within seconds the lethal projectiles passed him on all sides. He watched the arrows land behind the hoofs of his brothers' horses and then breathed a sigh of relief. He swung around, cocked the mechanism of his rifle again and raised the long weapon to

141

his shoulder.

The ear-splitting bullet had only just left his rifle barrel when he felt several sickening blows hit him in his side in quick succession.

As Delmer went to cock the Winchester again he suddenly realized what had just happened to him. He stared under his raised arm at the arrows which were skewered into him.

They had found their range, he thought as agonizing pain ripped through him. As the horse continued to pound across the sand he caught the taste of blood in his mouth.

Delmer summoned every scrap of his remaining strength and pushed his rifle's hand guard down. A brass casing flew from the magazine and floated into the distance. He was about to pull the hand guard back up when another arrow suddenly appeared through the darkness and hit him in his neck.

The outlaw buckled as blood poured from his mouth.

His Winchester flew up into the air as his gloved hands stiffened. Delmer's glazed eyes watched the rifle hit the sand and then looked up and stared helplessly at the approaching warriors.

The stricken outlaw fell from his saddle and crashed violently into the sand. With blood pouring from his hideous wounds, Delmer rolled over and over again as the Indians unshod ponies trampled over him.

The Indians raced after Caleb and Spike.

Their painted ponies tore through the eerie starlight and continued to chase the two remaining outlaws through the ocean of sand. The small muscular ponies were better suited to this parched terrain and quickly closed the distance between the saddle horses of their prey and themselves.

Caleb glanced at his brother and then stared into the darkness behind them as they tackled yet another dune. He reached out, grabbed Spike's bridle and drove his spurs into his own mount. The outlaw realized that Spike was more dead than alive and screamed at him.

'Wake the hell up, Spike,' he bellowed. 'I need your damn help. Wake up.'

His words fell on deaf ears.

As Caleb led his unconscious brother's mount up the dry shifting sand dune he suddenly became aware that Delmer was no longer keeping pace with them.

A chilling thought came to the outlaw. Without Delmer, Caleb knew that the odds of them surviving had become a lot slimmer.

Caleb pulled back on his reins and abruptly halted their horses. The loose sand shifted under the hoofs of their lathered-up mounts. He screwed up his sand-filled eyes and looked back into the black shadows.

'Delmer,' he shouted. 'Where in tarnation are you?'

Then he saw them. The determined warriors had circled the mountain of sand and were coming at him and his semi-conscious brother from all sides. As he held his horse in check he suddenly spotted something behind a few of the Indians. As the braves rode out of the shadows into the starlight, he spotted Delmer's saddle horse being led by one of the warriors.

Then Caleb saw something far more unnerving.

Delmer was draped lifelessly over the saddle of his mount. As the Indian led the horse into view Caleb could see blood sparkling in the starlight.

Caleb winced as he saw the arrows protruding from his brother's dead body. Engulfed in grief and anger, the outlaw pulled his guns and cocked their hammers.

'You bastards,' he feverishly shouted at the Indians. 'You done killed Delmer. I'll make you pay for that.'

Caleb started to fire but his bullets came too late.

Arrows flew into both the Holt brothers from every direction with venomous precision. Both Caleb and Spike were lifted off their saddles into the eerie

144

light and fell from their horses' backs.

The desert suddenly fell into a sickening silence.

The remaining warriors closed in on the Holt brothers' bodies and stared down at the last of the intruders. There was no sign of emotion on the faces of the young braves. They had simply done what they and their predecessors had always done and protected their scared ground.

As the outlaws' bodies lay on the sand, sparkling dark shadows spread out from their stricken forms. It pooled around the Holt brothers and glinted in the eerie illumination.

Even starlight could not lessen the horrific sight of blood as it spread from the crumpled outlaws.

FIFTEEN

The spectre that was Iron Eyes stood on the ledge above the chanting Indians with bullets in both hands and surveyed the scene like an eagle on a warm thermal observing its unsuspecting prey. Nothing escaped his bullet-coloured eyes as they watched as all preying creatures watch. He could still hear Squirrel Sally's voice cutting through the sound of drumbeats and intoxicated chanting.

It was either the late hour or the effects of the potent beverage they were consuming, but Iron Eyes had noticed that at least a quarter of the Indians had succumbed to sleep. His cold, calculating mind told him that he had to act now. There was no more time.

Iron Eyes lowered his head and then tossed the bullets out into the air and watched them fall into the centre of the campfire. The flames swept up around the ammunition as it rested in the heart of the inferno. He pushed a cigar between his teeth and scratched a match with his thumbnail as he waited for the inevitable.

He lit the end of the twisted cigar and sucked smoke into his emaciated body. Iron Eyes brooded and waited as smoke drifted back through his teeth.

The bounty hunter had lit the fuse and now he had to wait for the bullets to start exploding below him. He returned the cigar to his lips and inhaled the acrid smoke deeply and then adjusted the cutting rope in his hands.

His mind considered the shots he had heard echoing in the distance a few moments earlier. He wondered who else had made the mistake of venturing into this land. Whoever it had been was now silent. They had stopped firing their weaponry and there were only two reasons why that was so.

They had either won their short war or they had died trying. There was no other reason as far as the gaunt bounty hunter could figure.

After what had seemed like an eternity Iron Eyes tapped an inch of ash from the end of the cigar as the bullets began to start exploding below him. Iron Eyes glanced down and inhaled the familiar scent of gunsmoke as it rose with the flames.

Iron Eyes watched the random tapers of deadly

bullets shooting out of the massive fire. The red-hot bullets sped in all directions. Some hit the mountainside that he was standing upon. The sound of ricocheting bullets rang out as some of the lethal lead hit the rocks.

The Indians started to scatter hysterically. Those that were too slow were hit by his bullets emanating from the flames. Screams matched the sound of the ammunition.

No Fourth of July celebration could have equalled the bloody mayhem he had created. Iron Eyes pulled the cigar from his lips and tossed it away as he grabbed another handful of bullets from his pocket and threw them into the flames.

As the confusion spread like wildfire around the massive fire, Iron Eyes moved along the crumbling ledge until he found a firmer foothold.

Then he held on to the rope and leapt like a mountain lion away from the narrow ledge. Iron Eyes flew over the flames that licked at his coat tails. The rope tightened in his hands and pulled him back toward the cave mouth. Iron Eyes hurtled downward as bullets exploded beneath him and shot all around him.

Iron Eyes came speeding through the cloud of smoke like the devilish monster he resembled and hurtled toward the mouth of the cave. His bony hands then released his hold on the rope. He flew the last half dozen feet and landed on his mule-eared boots.

The momentum caused his thin body to run straight into the cave mouth to where Sally was spread-eagled on a smooth slab of stone.

No sooner had his boots hit the ground than his narrowed eyes saw the helpless Sally before him. A dozen or more Indians in their finery surrounded her. Some had knives drawn as though preparing to silence the fearless female.

His left hand drew one of his Navy Colts from his waistband and started firing at the warriors that were looming over her as his right pulled his Bowie knife from the neck of his boot.

Faster than he had ever moved before, the bounty hunter ran to the foot of the slab and swiftly cut the leather bonds around Sally's bare feet.

The startled Indians could not believe their eyes and were in total shock as the monstrous bounty hunter fired at them before they could turn their crude weaponry on the petite female.

With the deafening sound of exploding bullets behind his wide back, the notorious Iron Eyes used his empty gun to fight off the braves who were swinging their hatchets at him, and then with his long knife blade severed the leather laces that secured

149

Sally's hands.

Once the knife had achieved its goal, he slid it back into the neck of his boot and fended off the attacks of the few remaining Indians.

He thrashed his smoking gun across the skulls of the last remaining braves in the cave entrance and then moved to the side of Sally as she slid off the slab.

Another few Indians ran into the mouth of the cave with their hatchets raised. Iron Eyes pulled one of his razor-sharp spurs from his pocket and punched the first warrior across the jaw. As blood cascaded from the hideous wound, Iron Eyes grabbed the injured warrior and snapped his neck.

Sally swung one of the clubs she had salvaged from the dead Indians behind them and knocked the other Indians senseless.

Iron Eyes pushed his blood-soaked six-shooter into his trail coat pocket and then dragged its twin from his belt and resumed firing out of the cave. Within a matter of only seconds, the fearless bounty hunter had managed to free Sally and stop the Indians.

With blood dripping from the club in her hands, Sally nestled into the back of her saviour. She was shaking as the towering bounty hunter rested a shoulder against the cave wall.

Iron Eyes glanced down at her as the club fell from

her hand. He ruffled her hair and tried to look reassuring as he stared out at the campfire, which was still spewing bullets in every direction.

'We've gotta try and get out of here, Squirrel,' he said breathlessly. 'Trouble is there's a whole heap more of these critters outside this cave.'

With Sally at his side, Iron Eyes paused as his narrowed eyes studied the chaos he had caused. Bullets were still tearing from the massive fire in all directions as he thrust his gun into Sally's hands.

'Why'd you give me this?' Sally asked looking at the gun as smoke trailed from its long barrel.

'Just hold the damn thing while I reload, Squirrel,' Iron Eyes told her. 'I'm running low on notions of what to do next.'

'Ain't you got a plan, sweetheart?' she purred at the horrifically scarred man as he pushed the loaded six-gun into his belt and took the other from her hands.

He glanced briefly into her eyes and shrugged.

'Nope, I didn't expect to get this far, Squirrel,' Iron Eyes answered as his bony fingers removed the spent casings from the gun and then pushed fresh shells into the smoking cylinder. 'I figured they'd have killed me by now. Damned if I know what our next move oughta be.'

Sally frowned. 'What kinda plan is that?'

151

The tall bounty hunter shrugged before cocking the still hot six-shooter again. 'We're still living, Squirrel.'

'Where's my rifle?' Sally asked as Iron Eyes pulled the other Navy Colt and also cocked both it.

'I left it with my horse,' Iron Eyes replied as he inched closer to the vast expanse of sand.

'Where's your horse?' Sally pressed.

Iron Eyes looked down on the short female. 'He's over yonder passed them dunes. I didn't want to risk him getting shot by these Injuns.'

Sally looked angrily at the man who had just rescued her. 'You think more of that nag than you do of me, you ugly galoot.'

Iron Eyes nodded in agreement. 'That horse gets me out of trouble and you got a damn habit of getting me into it. Hell, gal. You're like human quick-sand.'

She clenched her fists and shook them under his nose.

'Why didn't you think of bringing my rifle, you dumb bastard?' she scolded. 'I'm plumb useless without it.'

Iron Eyes nodded.

'You're also a pain in the butt,' he added.

The area outside the mouth of the cave was filled with choking gunsmoke as his bullets still blasted

152

from the fire in sudden unpredictable bursts. The gaunt figure held his guns at hip level as he began to realize that he could use the dense smoke to shield them.

'C'mon, Squirrel. I got me an idea,' Iron Eyes grabbed her by the hair with his left gun hand and started to run. Her small legs somehow managed to keep pace with his lengthy strides. As warriors appeared with raised weapons, Iron Eyes swung on his hips and shot them. The fearsome figure did not miss a step.

As the pair ran through the dense smoke, Sally looked up into his face. He was shooting at anyone who looked as though they might try and slow their progress.

'Where in tarnation are we going, you sorrowful daddy-long-legs?' Sally yelled out as the bounty hunter shielded her behind the tails of his long coat and fired at two charging braves. Both were knocked off their feet by the power of his bullets.

Iron Eyes grabbed hold of Sally and threw her over a pile of sand. She landed on her ample rump and winced.

Without speaking, he pointed behind her. Sally turned and saw her team of black horses tethered close to countless Indian ponies.

'My team,' she gushed as she scrambled to her feet

and rushed toward them. 'Where's my stagecoach?'

Iron Eyes fired another two shots into the floating smoke and then swung on his heels and rushed to her side. He then pushed his guns into his coat pockets and unceremoniously lifted her off her feet and dropped her on to the back of one of the black horses.

'Where's my damn stagecoach?' Sally repeated as Iron Eyes hastily moved between the sturdy animals and made sure that they were all tethered together.

Iron Eyes grabbed the mane of another of the horses and swung his painfully lean frame on to its back. As he sat on the muscular animal he fastened his spurs to his boots and then looked at his companion.

'Will you hush the hell up, woman,' he riled.

Sally blushed as though her betrothed had flattered her by calling her a woman. 'You sure are tetchy.'

'I got me a good reason to be tetchy, Squirrel,' he shouted and then thrust his spurs into the animal beneath him. The entire team raced through the billowing gunsmoke as more bullets cut through the air from the flaming fire. 'First we'll pick up my palomino and then head on to your stage.'

The team of six black horses ploughed through anything that got in their way as the gaunt bounty hunter and the golden-haired female hung on to the yokes of the horses and steered them clear of the Indians' stronghold.

FINALE

It was still dark as Iron Eyes secured the last of the team's chains and leathers to the wooden traces. He moved silently back to the stagecoach as Sally climbed back up to the driver's box and carefully adjusted the long reins in her tiny hands. She grinned down at the bounty hunter as he pulled her Winchester from under his saddle and threw it up to her. Sally caught the long rifle and rested it on her ragged pants.

'You're awful quiet, you ugly galoot,' Sally teased as the silent bounty hunter circled the stagecoach to check that everything was OK. 'Ain't you gonna speak to me?'

Iron Eyes glanced at her, but said nothing. He looked at the sky and then picked his reins off the sand and moved closer to the palomino stallion.

Sally looked frustrated as she found her pipe and poked its stem in the corner of her mouth as she rested the rifle across her lap.

'What's wrong, Iron Eyes?' she asked. 'Is it 'coz I ain't thanked you for saving my bacon? OK, thanks.'

His eyes glanced at her and then he stepped into his stirrup and hoisted his lean frame up. His right leg cleared his silver saddle horn and then he gently lowered himself down on his ornate saddle. As he did so she noticed him wince.

'Is that wound on your side giving you trouble, lover?' Sally asked with genuine concern in her voice. 'Is it?'

He stared across the distance between his handsome horse and her high perch on the stagecoach.

'Nope,' he eventually answered as he gathered up his reins and slowly turned the palomino. 'We'd best get out of here before we tangle with any more of them damn Injuns. It'll be light in about an hour.'

Sally looked confused. She struck a match and sucked its flame into the bowl of her pipe as she studied her beloved. As smoke drifted from her mouth, she rested a foot on the brake pole and watched him.

'Something's wrong, Iron Eyes,' she stated firmly. 'I ain't gonna stop asking until you tell me what it is. What the hell is wrong with you?'

Iron Eyes moved his high-shouldered horse closer and looked up at her. He sighed heavily and shook his head.

'You sure are a real nag, Squirrel,' he said.

'I know that,' she grinned. 'What I don't know is why you're all grumpy with me. Spill them beans.'

Iron Eyes pushed his lank hair off his face.

'You know when I threw them bullets into that campfire?' he asked. 'It seemed like a real good idea at the time.'

'It was a good idea,' Sally confirmed. 'It distracted them long enough for you to rescue me. How come that's got you so moody?'

'Them bullets were firing wild, Squirrel,' he frowned and then pointed at his rump. 'They were shooting in every damn direction.'

Sally looked to where he was indicating and started to grin wider than she had ever grinned before. The torn fabric of his pants was quite clear as he started his horse moving.

'That's your own fault,' Sally scoffed. 'You said that I was a pain in the rump. Now you know what a real pain in the rump is.'

Iron Eyes sighed. 'Very funny.'

'You got shot in the ass by one of your own bullets?' she roared as she whipped her team into action and released her brake. 'That'll teach you.'

'Not shot, Squirrel,' Iron Eyes corrected over his shoulder. 'I got grazed.'

'I bet it's sore,' Sally laughed.

He stared at her through his limp black locks.

'You trouble me, Squirrel,' he snarled as he found a whiskey bottle in his saddle-bags and took a swig. 'You really trouble me.'

'Not as much as that damn bullet does, darling,' she laughed out loud and lashed her long leathers across the backs of her striding team.